0264015

172

Is it the sun, Philibert?

Also by Roch Carrier

Jolis deuils (Editions du jour)
La guerre, yes Sir! (Editions du jour)
Contes pour mille oreilles (Ecrits du Canada Français)
Floralie, où est-tu? (Editions du jour)
La guerre, yes Sir! (Dramatic version — Editions du jour)
Il est par là, le soleil (Editions du jour)

in translation

La Guerre, Yes Sir!
Floralie, Where Are You?

Is it the sun, Philibert?

Roch Carrier

translated by Sheila Fischman

Toronto   Anansi   1972

Il est par là, le soleil was first published in 1970
by Editions du Jour, 1651 rue Saint-Denis, Montréal.

Published with the assistance of the Canada Council.

Cover design by Roland Giguère

ISBN: 0 88784 321 2(paper); 0 88784 420 0(cloth)
Library of Congress Card Number: 75-190705

1 2 3 4 5   76 75 74 73 72
Printed in Canada by The Hunter Rose Company

House of Anansi Press Ltd.
471 Jarvis Street
Toronto, Canada

This story is dedicated to those who never told it

because they wanted to forget.

Translator's Foreword

Is it the sun, Philibert? completes the trilogy that began with *La Guerre, Yes Sir!*, then skipped back a generation or so to *Floralie, Where Are You?* While the first two novels took place over long, drawn-out nights, here most of a lifetime is telescoped into a few pages. And while the first two novels had a rural setting, where the snow was so white it took a war to leave a stain on it, here the setting is Montreal, where in the first few pages Philibert, son of the grave-digger in *La Guerre, Yes Sir!*, finds the snow an unfamiliar element that tastes of mud.

It's not just the snow that makes Montreal a hostile environment for Philibert. His first encounters with the legendary English-speaking minority are devastating and in another personality might have marked the beginnings of political awareness. But, although there are some resemblances to the real life of Pierre Vallières, Philibert would never think of himself as a "white nigger," or even as a Québécois. He considers himself, rather, "un petit Canadien-français" and a born loser, destined always to suffer at the hands of "les gros" — who might comprise anyone from "le boss" (who might speak any one of a number of languages, including French) to God himself. Philibert does take some steps towards rejecting his traditional role. By openly declaring his loss of faith and by changing newspapers, forsaking *Montréal-Matin*, house-organ of the then-ruling Union-Nationale party, for *La Presse*, he rejects two powerful institutions of the Québec of the forties and fifties.

He does not question the need to learn English to help advance himself, and in one of the novel's more poignant moments, when Philibert at last has a job that promises him a measure of self-respect, his first impulse is to change his name, to call himself "Mister Phil." Duddy Kravitz became Dudley Kane too, but Philibert is no Duddy Kravitz. His life is a series of put-downs and failures and his dreams of success seem sadly misdirected. "Philibert did not understand" is a recurring complaint. Duddy Kravitz understood only too well.

Readers of *La Guerre, Yes Sir!* should have no trouble understanding the curses and swearing here. The litany is much the same, with some emphasis on "ciboire" (ciborium) as a term of insult. Just as Anglo-Saxon four-letter words are rarely decorated with asterisks, many Québec oaths are written out as pronounced, as "crisse" or "tabernaque," for example. Roch Carrier prefers to emphasize the original intent of these blasphemies and to write them in their proper form.

Roch Carrier sees this account of one not untypical life as representative of what he calls the last third of Québec's dark ages. And, as in the earlier novels, he has used his incomparable humour to make it palatable, to himself as well as to his readers. Its ambiguous conclusion and title are suggestive of many more questions, not just for Philibert but for all the "petits Canadien-français — and for the Québécois as well as for the *Anglais, maudits* or otherwise. Philibert's story, like those that preceded it, may be at least as helpful as many official reports in understanding various public events and personalities. And certainly more entertaining.

— S.F.

Philibert would never forget the sound the crumpled paper made, green paper with gaily-coloured designs, pictures of snow, little red men, deer and spruce trees with lights on them. His mother saved it from year to year, smoothing it out with her iron and storing it away for the next Christmas. He had found a box wrapped in Christmas paper in the dust under his parents' bed. Wait until Christmas Eve to open it . . . but Philibert could not wait. He ripped open the package. In his impatient fingers the paper made a noise he would remember for the rest of his life. In the box there was a toy car. Philibert picked it up and ran happily to the kitchen to give his mother a kiss. His father grabbed him by the arm ("That toy's for Christmas. Not before."), snatched

5

the toy away from him, threw it on the floor and stomped on it with that big leather boot of his that made the stairs tremble, and the ceiling on its axe-hewn beams; that big foot that could dig a hole in the snow big enough to hold Philibert like a grave.

"No! No!" cried the child.

The man opened the door and threw the flattened toy into the snow.

"In this life you got to learn to wait for things," the big voice told him.

The child looked for the remains of his toy in the falling snow. The car was lost. It was useless to crawl around and look for it, digging through the snow with his swollen hand.

Christmas drew near, like the muzzle of a wolf. There would be no present for Philibert. But under the tree, among the brightly-coloured boxes, there was a tag with his name on it. He tore frantically at the paper. The rustling sound delighted him.

The box was empty.

It was the box that had contained the toy car.

Every day he dug in the snow, looking for the lost toy. When spring came he examined the melting snow, waiting, hoping. But when the yellow grass appeared he was forced to admit that even though it was impossible, the toy had melted with the snow.

*　　*　　*

Every year, when the stubble in the fields was white with the first frosts and the trees' crooked fingers came through the windows to scratch at the walls and grapple with Philibert's blankets, a man with long boots and a red runny nose came to tell him a story, always the same one.

"This morning I was walking along the river, in there where the little trees are, you know, like little balls of needles. Nothing but branches; no more leaves. They whip at your face, those little branches. They're all stiff like porcupine quills. All of a sudden, what do I see but thirty-nine ducks. I could count them because they weren't moving. They were stuck in the river because the river was all frozen over. Just their necks were sticking out: thirty-nine heads squirming around and thirty-nine quacking beaks. Arsène, can you see yourself stuck in the river like that with nothing but your beard showing over the top? Philibert, can you see yourself, little fellow? "

The ice squeezes the ducks and pulls out their feathers. Their heads are drooping flowers.

The old hunter goes to look for a weapon and comes back to the river with a scythe as though he were going to cut grass. At this time of year! With one great swath he slices off several heads and they go skittering along the ice. The old man strikes out again and cuts more heads, which slide across the ice as they fall until finally they stop in their own frozen blood.

When his crimson harvest is complete the man takes an axe to cut, around the birds, the ice which is already softening in the autumn sun.

7

That night the sliced-off heads appeared like sorrowful stars. Red stars that cried out in the silence and bled onto Philibert. They slithered across the floor of his bedroom like snails, climbed into his bed and got tangled in his sheets.

*   *   *

His parents' bed creaked and groaned like a buggy on a bumpy road, behind the imperfectly joined green boards of the dividing wall. Every night Philibert was awakened by the noisy clamour in which his father and mother fell silent and even their breathing seemed to stop. Only the bed complained, creaking and crying, a tortured beast in the night.

*   *   *

The child was peacefully digging a little hole next to his father, who was preparing a grave for the coffin of one of the villagers. When the big hole had been dug his father went off through the muddy earth towards a little white cabin at the back of the graveyard. Three or four coffins had been piled up there since winter, waiting for spring to soften the ground so they could be buried. Winter keeps dead men stiff and odourless.

His father pulled out a coffin, loaded it onto his wheelbarrow and tossed it into the hole which he hastily filled in with shovelfuls of dirt, as though he wanted to have it forgotten under the ground. What was there for

Philibert to bury? The coffins in the white cabin were too big. Only his father could move them, and it was hard even for him. His face turned all red, the big muscles swelling in his neck, and he puffed like a horse. Philibert had noticed a white coffin, smaller than the others: the coffin of a child. He would make the grave he was digging a little bigger and put the white coffin in it. He was able to lift one end of the coffin and he could feel the small corpse sliding around inside it — was it the head or the feet that had struck against the inner wall? — but he could not lift the coffin all the way off the ground.

He went back to his little grave rather sadly and knelt down. He put his hand at the bottom and threw some dirt over it, saying that his hand was dead, the worms were eating it up, that his hand was rotting, it was damned, the fire of hell with all its shiny teeth was devouring his hand and it would suffer eternally. The child raised his other hand to his mouth, curled his fingers to make a trumpet, puffed out his cheeks and blew.

"Toot, toot, toot, ta-ta toot, toota, toota . . ."

It was the trumpet of the Last Judgment. The dead began to stir beneath the ground like dreamers clutching at the last remnants of sleep before it fled. Philibert pulled his hand out of the ground. It had not rotted. It was not pitted with worm-holes, nor had it been marked by fiery fangs. His hand was as new as the other one.

Next to him, his father pushed aside some dirt. It fell onto the coffin with a heavy thump. He was humming, unaware that the dead were stirring under their blanket of earth. He sang as he filled in the grave.

Philibert ran to the house, took a doll out of the box that served as its bed and went back to the graveyard. He ran among the white crosses and black epitaphs. Then he laid the doll on the floor of the grave, used his little shovel to cover it with dirt, and was finished at the same time as his father, who had filled in a man-sized grave. Philibert made a cross out of two bits of branch. His sister, in tears, was looking for her baby.

Philibert was happy. It was just like a real funeral.

* * *

"Mama! Mama! I'm dreaming!"

The silence and the night had big hairy hands that pressed on his neck. Philibert was trembling, afraid. He got up, staggering with sleep. The earth beneath his feet was eternally still. He moved his hand towards some tall plants, but the stems and flowers and bushes and thorns slipped away as though they had turned to night. He looked for his village. He broke into a run. Tripped. Ran. His breathing was in the mouth of someone behind him. He climbed up the night as though he were going against a current. He walked. Ran. His village was no longer there. Nor the mountain. Nor the smell of fresh bread. The child was searching in the tall grasses of night as though he had lost a ball.

In the place where all the houses in the village came together there was only his father, tall and strong, throwing the last shovelfuls of dirt onto a coffin. The stirred-up earth formed a lump that he flattened with his big feet. In the cool black night his father too was all black: face, hands and clothes. The sweat on his forehead was black as well. His father had buried the whole village.

"Mama! I'm having a bad dream!"

"Shut up!"

*   *   *

Philibert and his father were running through the snow trying to catch a pig. They laughed at the ridiculous mass of lard trying to make itself agile, running away from them as it wept like a baby. The creature got stuck in the snow. Philibert and his father, taking their time, climbed on the pig's back to immobilize it. Seated there they were like two mad kings on a throne. Taking hold of an ear, the father planted his big knife in the neck of screaming flesh and the blood sprayed his face. The entire field turned red and the snow remained the colour of blood until the next storm. The pig squealed loud enough to burst God's eardrums, but the laughter of Philibert and his father was louder still. The pig seemed to grow silent only when it had been stretched out on a vertical ladder, its belly split open and its insides all cleaned out.

"It's got to be as clean as a nun's bum," said the father.

The boiling water was steaming away, sizzling on the animal's belly. And sometimes at night, when the wind was blowing, Philibert heard it cry.

On slaughter days his father talked in the morning at breakfast time, between spoonfuls of porridge which he gulped down with a grunt. On those days Arsène never beat the children. When he came back in the evening, his hands all red, if he did run after the squealing children it was not to slap them. His favourite would receive as a gift the animal's frozen tail, slipped into his shirt by a big cold red hand.

Arsène would have liked to find a job where he just had to kill pigs or cows, or any other animal for that matter. One day he asked his wife to write to an abattoir in Chicago to ask the head slaughterer if he might need the help of the best pig-sticker in the Appalachian Townships.

"There's no future in this country. You can't kill ten pigs a day. You got to have more people getting married or more people dying. Either that or we need a war. There's one going on but it's in the Old Countries so we've got peace here; but if I was ten years younger and I didn't have so many kids I think I'd have got on the train and gone away to fight that war in the Old Countries."

*　*　*

Philibert loved to watch the cut-off tongue on the floor. It was still. It had bristles. Then all of a sudden it would contract. It was the movement Philibert had been waiting for, but he was still startled to see the evidence of life in the dead tongue. It curled up, uncurled, seemed to want to have a life of its own, to go off and leap like a toad, perhaps turn around in the pig's mouth or run away as far as the horizon or fly off into the sky. Philibert stepped back; that tongue could very well leap up into his face and go right into his mouth. But it stayed on the big worn-out floorboards. It quivered and trembled and shook. Philibert was fascinated, but even though he was used to it he could not help being afraid. Every time the tongue was shaken by a contraction it was a sign of life that was not life, because the pig had had its throat cut.

In the big voice that whistled through his yellow teeth and spread out over his three-day beard, his father said, "Listen, son. The tongue's talking. Can you hear it?"

"What's it saying?"

"What do you thing it's saying? Prayers? It's talking dirty: pig-talk."

A burst of laughter split his father's face. It started at his feet and shook and inundated his whole body. Words appeared on his lips and flowed back into his laughter. Later, the child would understand.

Philibert sat down in front of the pig's tongue and tried to understand its language. Each tremor contained a word. He listened. The tongue spoke, dirty words. The pig's tongue cursed like a man. Seated in front of the tongue, his chin in his hands, Philibert listened for hours to the pig's tongue uttering tremendous oaths, oaths that would make the ground tremble, they resounded so deeply into hell. The tongue uttered everything it knew about what men and women do together in their beds at night, or in the hay or straw.

"Christ!" said the pig's tongue.

Philibert repeated the word from the depths of his soul. When he was a man he would be entitled to swear out loud, to curse as loud as he wanted, like his father and all the other men. He wouldn't have to go and hide in the bushes at the end of the field when he wanted to insult the saints in Heaven.

"Tits," said the tongue.

Philibert thought of the dark dizzying pit he had seen in the opening of Madame Joseph's dress in church on Sunday when she bent over to genuflect.

Philibert listened for hours to the tongue uttering forbidden words, hoping that one day he would be a man. Then the words became gradually more widely spaced, the tongue was frozen in silence and it stopped moving. He was sad. Silence stopped his own tongue.

* * *

It was an old wooden house, always repainted white to erase the years. Philibert loved it, because in order to reach it he had to go along a dirt path that was almost a secret path. It disappeared beneath the willow leaves like an egg under a hen. When the light of day had left a bitter taste in his mouth Philibert would set off towards the house, walking under the canopy of fragrant leaves that sang softly for him, making the day fresh again.

With rough, resin-scented words his grandfather would reconstruct the past and the child Philibert shivered with the delight of being alive so that when he was old enough he too would be able to tell stories that would make children long for old age.

Today the hand of sadness weighed heavily on his back. He went towards the old wooden house. He recognized the road, the pebbles. The tracks of passing cars in the mud were a writing that he knew. But the willows had disappeared. It was as though they had gone back into the earth from which they had sprung long before Grandfather was a child.

The willows had been cut down.

The grass was pale, deprived of their green shade, and at the end of the denuded lane his grandparents' house seemed ashamed of its poor peeling wood. Rats had gnawed around the base of the house. One day it would tumble down. There would be no more willows to give the wood of the house the desire not to die.

Troubled and uncomprehending, Philibert pushed at the door as cautiously as though he were entering an unknown house. His fingers were clenched with anguish on the handle, which creaked because of the rust. Inside, his grandparents were sitting in their usual places, in their chairs that danced like ships on the seas of the past. Grandmother was embroidering a cushion; she said she was making a sky. Grandfather spat. There were pigs nosing about in the room. Philibert was amazed. He wanted to leave. One pig was dozing silently, leaning against a door. Another was tumbling down the stairs and its weight made the house shake.

"We were young once," said Grandfather.

"We were young like you," said Grandmother.

"We were younger than you."

"Now we're old."

"So, to give us something to leave behind for our children to inherit when we die, we sold the house."

"I had seventeen children in this house. It was in this very house that our children became men and women . . ."

"Nuns, a priest, farmers . . . a salesman, soldiers."

"Or they died."

"We loved it, this house of ours. When we bought it, it was already old."

"But it got younger because we were young."

"We were young . . . we loved our house."

"We sold it because our children are pretty fond of money."

"And inheritances."

Grandfather looked for matches so he could relight his pipe.

"They turned our house into a pigsty," the old lady muttered.

"But you get used to pigs."

"And you get used to growing old."

"But we haven't finished living yet."

Grandfather stood up. "Either they're going to get rid of their pigs or they'll have to get rid of my cold carcass."

He climbed up on his chair, pulled his shotgun off the wall where it was held by two nails. He opened the window and fired a shot, startling the animals.

"We want to live," said Grandfather.

"What's the good of living?" asked Grandmother.

*   *   *

Here comes the procession. Under the polished Sunday shoes the street was quiet. The sun was caught in the monstrance that the Curé held at the level of his head so it seemed to be made of sparkling gold. God was proceeding through the village and his light was gleaming over the silence of the dazzled roofs. The green of the leaves became more intense and the oats bent piously and swayed. Jonas Laliberté and his wife walked behind the Curé, their eyes closed. They were not so lacking in respect as to dare to look at God. Behind them, accompanied by their godfathers and godmothers, followed their twenty-one children. The youngest was closest to the monstrance and the eldest was the farthest away. Each day that one lives makes one less worthy to be close to God. The wheels of twenty-one wheelbarrows in which the twenty-one children were being transported turned with no sound from the axles, no noise of pebbles under the rims of the wheels. The wheelbarrows floated along in the light that carried

17

them. The children were silent. Arms hung down from each wheelbarrow. Each one was filled not with a body but with a sloppy, spreading formless paste, where a head with lifeless eyes and a blissful smile floated. The big round heads would have tumbled outside the wheelbarrows and dragged the boneless bodies as they fell if they had not been held back by the godmothers' pious hands.

Jonas Laliberté and his wife murmured prayers. They owed much to God, who could have withheld his blessing from their union by giving them only a few children. But God in his wisdom had chosen to give many children to Jonas Laliberté. Jonas and his wife were grateful. They had been chosen to be the protectors of twenty-one little angels, chosen by God in his Heaven to represent his justice and goodness on earth. Jonas and his wife gave fervent thanks. If he had wanted, all-powerful God could have withdrawn the breath of life from these children who had been born as soft as cream, so the Curé had explained, but in the greatness of his divine wisdom, which is incomprehensible to mortals, God had breathed a tenacious life into these little angels whom he had created crippled so that they would receive a greater love. Jonas Laliberté and his wife murmured Hail Mary's to let God know that their gratitude was complete.

In the village street, which the women had swept clean in preparation for the divine visit, following behind God in his monstrance, the godfathers pushed the twenty-one wheelbarrows filled with faccid flesh, with enormous heads, with a tangle of wobbly arms. They carried the children that had come each year to remind Jonas Laliberté that God does not forget his faithful servant, but entrusts to him the most difficult tasks. The godfathers gripped the handles with great care. If the wheelbarrows had been held less firmly the bodies of liquid flesh would have spilled to the ground like dirty water.

Philibert approached the road, a blade of grass between his teeth. He wanted to watch the procession go by. He wished he could be taken for a ride in a wheelbarrow like those worms with children's heads. But nobody ever took him for a walk. He was condemned always to walk on his own two legs. It wasn't fair that others always had people to take them for walks. He hated those monsters.

After the twenty-one Laliberté children came some hunchbacks, then the ones with clubfeet and those with one leg shorter than the other, followed by the maimed: those who had stopped a circular saw with their bellies, those who had whacked themselves in the knee with an axe, those with the print of a horseshoe on the forehead, those who had had a leg crushed under a tree, those who had frozen a finger during the winter, those who had been cut in the legs by a scythe, those with one bad eye. Finally, walking heavily, but submissive to the will of God, came the widows all in black, walking as though they were tired. All were singing:

Jesus, Jesus, Lord and King,
Jesus who turns the black winter to spring,
Jesus who gives us everything,
Jesus, Jesus, Jesus Lord,
Christ, have pity on me!
Yes, Christ have pity on me!

The rest of the procession dragged on in silence.
The old men and women, the mark of death already
erasing their features, walked slowly, their bent backs
no doubt supporting an invisible burden, their unbearable memories.

Holding himself slightly apart from the others
because he did not dare to close up the few steps that
separated him from the procession, the child Philibert
followed, not praying, and the pebbles pushed along by
his foot were not silent. They rippled the silence of the
pious ceremony like water.

The cortège followed the path that led to the
villages on the plain. The child walked in the field that
skirted the road, capering along without letting the
distance between him and the others increase too much.
He caught grasshoppers, pulled off their legs and threw
the impotent little creatures into the oats. The sun, still
very high, embraced the earth in its rays. The silence of
the cortège was gently transformed into a long plaint,
long as the sad wind above the oatfield.

*   *   *

Philibert, wearing clothes of his father's that were too big for him, was in a hurry. He was running away. He had already forgotten what he was leaving behind. He had forgotten the effort he expended at every step as he sank to his belly in the snow. He soared like a bird, all his wings offered up to the wind. Everything was erased by the snow. He no longer remembered his father and he had already forgotten his mother. The village was covered in snow. His memory was a white plain that stretched as far as the eye could see and his footprints were the first marks of a new life. His bony adolescent body was too narrow to contain his soul.

At each beat his heart said, "Farther, farther," and all down the length of his veins his blood repeated this word that rose to his mouth like a cry.

* * *

The truck stopped. Philibert woke up. The big man behind the wheel gave him a push, laughing. Philibert jumped, but there was nothing for his feet to dig into. He was in the middle of a street. The snow was brown. He raised his eyes and it looked to him as though ten villages had been thrown down, piled on top of each other with all their houses and churches and cars and old men. One day it would all collapse; the windows would break, the walls would tumble down, the bricks would rot one by one like apples on a tree. The streets would writhe and the old men would try to escape but

21

they would be run over by the cars. He felt a pitchfork in his belly: hunger.

The walls receded before his eyes as though they were floating. The snow tasted of mud. People were walking behind one another, colliding, their heads pulled down between their shoulders. They were bushy, living overcoats. A door was open in front of him. Would he go in? A bit of warmth caressed his face. He would go in. He didn't dare. Where would this bus take him, anyway? He wouldn't get on it. The bus would take him some place and he would never come back. But it was warm.

"Why don't they build their goddamn cities like villages? Then maybe we wouldn't get lost."

He would not get on the bus. He would retrace his steps, find another truck and go back to where he came from.

"No, *baptême,* I won't go back to the village!"

The driver at the wheel motioned him to get on. He was getting impatient.

Philibert shook his head to indicate that he was not getting on, but he stayed in the doorway. The driver smiled. Philibert guessed that the man did not possess a spark of kindness.

The door closed again. The bus shot forward with Philibert wedged between the two halves of the door, his head inside and his feet, kicking, on the outside. The bus moved on, smug as a cat with a mouse in its jaws.

"Open up, *baptême!* Wherever it is you're going, I don't want to go."

With a broad grin, almost kind, the driver explained, taking his hands off the wheel to make elaborate gestures, "It's free. There's just the King and the Pope that gets a free ride. And you."

In the bus there were heads sticking out of coats. The faces were broad and they neither smiled nor slept. They simply swayed with the motion of the bus.

"Let me off, *baptême!* I want to walk on my own two feet."

The faces glistened like the dough for the *tourtières* when his mother brushed melted butter over them. The driver's smile had nothing good in it.

"May the good Lord stick a cauliflower up your ass and the devil put cabbage worms in it!"

He burst into tears in the yoke of the two door-halves closed on either side of his neck. His jacket was pulled off his shoulders, but there was no more cold in the Montreal winter.

He hated his clothes with their smell of the stable.

Philibert would be as ruthless as he had to in order to survive.

The doors opened abruptly, the bus came to a stop and Philibert was ejected into the mud. He was on his knees, but he was not praying. He wasn't swearing either. He was hungry. He shook his hands to get rid of the mud and slush. The windows, like the faces all around him, were indifferent. Hunger was devouring him like a voracious rat. He had eaten snow all along the way, but in Montreal the snow was too dirty. If it were summer he would have browsed on the grass. No; there wasn't any grass in Montreal. Philibert saw nothing but walls and streets and a few passers-by bent over in the brown snow.

His feet were floating in a muddy stream.

Montreal smelled of oil. Cars screeched as they drove along. It smelled like a garage.

The houses seemed to be walking in every direction beside him.

* * *

There was a shovel stuck in the snow. He picked it up, slung it over his shoulder and took off. He ran among the men and women who were walking along with their heads in their scarves. Farther away, much farther, he stopped. He began to clear the sidewalk that led up to one of the houses, heaving big shovelfuls of snow. The snow wasn't muddy here. It was a white powder, where children could slide and roll and go to sleep. They could eat it or hide in it. But Philibert didn't see any children. The snow had a smell that was carried to his face by the wind. It was the smell of ashes. When he had finished digging the passage through the snow he would ask for what he had coming to him and go and find something to eat. There was a strength in his arms that would never have come to him if his father had asked him for help. Each shovelful of snow that he moved from the front of this house was as important as one of his heartbeats.

Then at last the path was cleared. The sidewalk looked nicely grey at the bottom of the trench he had cut through the snow.

He hesitated before the big oak door. But he was hungry.

A light was turned on behind the square of opaque glass. The door was opened part way. Philibert pushed. The round head of a little old man shone in the doorway.

"Shovel your walk for a quarter," said Philibert, holding out his hand.

"No beggars." In English.

He was pushed back by the heavy door. He hadn't understood a word the old man muttered.

"*Vieux Christ!* If you drop dead it won't be me that buries you."

With his shovel and his feet he put back all the snow he had removed from the sidewalk.

How much longer would he have to carry around that fiery stone in his belly?

In front of the neighbouring house he set to once more, attacking the accumulated snow. The sidewalk was long; the house was set back a long way from the street. In summer, when the leaves had not all been devoured by winter, the house must be hidden in whispering green music.

The shovelled walk looked like a very clean rug laid down over the white snow. When he knocked at the door he sensed someone moving behind it, but it wasn't opened. It was as still as a stone wall. He waited some

25

more, then went away without throwing the snow back onto the clean sidewalk.

A little farther on, Philibert dug another path. His jacket was as wet as though it were raining, but his sweat turned to ice and he could feel the cold stiff weight of the wool against his back. He knocked at the door. A dog growled. He waited. No one came and the dog growled again.

Philibert threw his shovel as far as he could. He was hungry. Who would give him something to eat? He would steal, he would rob somebody. But before he did that he would try to earn a few cents. His father used to say, "It's easier to earn the first cent than the first million." Philibert had no desire to be rich. He just wanted to be able to eat. He went back to look for his shovel, stuck in the snow. His boots were filled with water from the snow melting around his icy ankles.

Would he have to clean the snow off all the streets in Montreal before he found something to eat? Philibert pushed his shovel into the snow, lifted the fragile blocks which the wind blew into flakes, and threw them as far as he could. The shovel made a small rough noise as it sank in, then leaped out like an animal that bit at the snow and leaped and bit and leaped along with the sighs that came from Philibert's chest. And then the walk was clean. Philibert rushed to knock at the door. It opened.

"No. No. Sorry." In English again.

The door was shut in his face, like a slap. He wanted to cry. But where could he stop to cry? What could he lean against to let the tears pour out until all the sorrow had been drained from his body?

He was hungry.

In this part of town there wasn't even any garbage lying around. There weren't even any frozen crusts thrown out on the snow for the birds. He looked around for cigarette butts, but these people were very clean and Philibert couldn't put off his hunger by chewing tobacco.

The street stretched out ahead of him; it walked too, just like him. The wall of silent houses appeared on only one side now. On the other side, behind the pillars of some naked trees, a snowy deserted park stretched out. The shovel on his shoulder, Philibert crossed the street where cars moved along very politely. He climbed over the iron fence. The ice in his clothes no longer tormented him. He smiled. For the moment his hunger was asleep in his belly. Playing in the snow like a child he started to write: with a surge of joy, laughing wildly, with a strength that would sear the concrete, Philibert stamped in the snow as hard as he could, spelling out letters, words, a whole sentence that stretched from one end of the park to the other, as though it were a white page. Then he jumped over the fence and into the street.

And behind the shadow of a window, an old lady with a string of pearls around her neck read in the snow words she could not understand. They said: YOU HAVE AN ASSHOLE INSTEAD OF A HEART.

* * *

Suddenly the door in front of him was open. He didn't dare take a step. But the door stayed open. He moved one foot forward, one back. He barely moved at all. The door stayed open and the lady standing in the doorway spoke to him. He didn't understand her.

"If you talked French like everybody else maybe I'd know what you were saying."

"Oh! Poor boy. You don't speak English. . . Are you an Italian?"

And her strange accent made it sound like "an Italienne," an Italian girl. Philibert looked at her, bewildered.

"An Italian girl? *Baptême* no, I ain't an Italian girl. That's the most insulting thing I ever heard." Philibert turned, intending to leave.

The lady put her hand on his arm. He was a dirty, smelly little tramp with drops of ice on his face, but she could not let him go without helping him. His eyes were red and sunk deep in their sockets from exhaustion. He was so pale and his clothes looked so big for him.

God is cruel indeed, thought the lady, if he tosses these poor abandoned dogs into the streets of Montreal. Their parents must be unspeakable if they let their children run away so young instead of making a fuss over them. These children were too young to know life's hardships. This young man, for example: had he eaten today? And he couldn't even speak English. What a pity! These immigrants should learn the language before they set off for Canada. Could he be Yugoslavian, or perhaps Hungarian?

She looked at the young man at her door, pitiful as he was, but she saw only her son. He had been the same age when he left, laughing, his duffle-bag over his shoulder.

"Don't expect me home for supper, Mom! " he had said. He left with the Royal Air Force. He did not come back. But his death had contributed to the liberation of Europe. He had not died in vain.

The lady's eyes, fixed on him, reminded Philibert of his mother's. She had often looked at him with her eyes full of all kinds of things she seemed to see around him.

"Come in!"

As he did not understand she took away his shovel and leaned it against a wall, then, taking his arm, she led him down a long hallway that went into the kitchen. She pushed him towards the table and pointed to a chair. Philibert snatched a bun out of a basket. She poured him some tea. Philibert took another bun and shoved the whole thing into his mouth. The lady burst out laughing.

"You goddamn woman, if you're going to laugh at me I'm taking everything I can eat and getting the hell out. So long!"

The lady held him back with one hand on his shoulder. She said something to him; he could tell from the tone of her voice that she was not making fun of him. He swallowed his cup of tea in one gulp. She poured him another and brought more buns. Philibert enjoyed the sensation of the moist chewy paste in his mouth. The lady laughed as she spoke some more incomprehensible words. He replied "Yes sir," to everything she said. He didn't know any other English words. She laughed, but without making any sound. She only opened her lips. She seemed to be afraid of laughing. Philibert wanted to say something dirty, four or five oaths that would rear up in the kitchen like great bears. But she wouldn't understand them so he kept quiet. Beneath the embroidery of her dressing-gown her large bosom seemed to have been carved from warm stone.

He was still hungry when the basket was empty but the lady did not notice. How could he ask for more buns and make himself understood?

"Yum yum! Yes sir!"

The lady puffed out her cheeks and her eyes sparkled behind the narrow slit of her eyelids. She poured him some tea which he drank, forgetting that he would have preferred to eat.

"Poor child . . ."

She was saying words he did not understand.

"Yes sir," he replied.

The lady guided him towards another room and opened the door. It was a bathroom like the ones he had seen in the newspaper. Turning the taps at random he felt a rush of cold water on his shoulder. He yelled with surprise. The lady called from the other side of the door. His jacket was all wet and the bathtub was full to the brim. He turned off the tap, undressed, stepped back, sprang forward and jumped in, just the way he used to jump into the Famine River.

The lady was knocking frantically on the other side of the door.

"Don't bust it down, you old bag," shouted Philibert. "Yes sir!"

The lady came in carrying a pile of folded towels under her arm. She put them on the floor one by one to soak up the water, rubbing them around with her feet, but she kept one in her hands. This towel, a blue one, she unfolded and wrapped around Philibert's shoulders. He was enveloped in a gentle fire, spread over his back by a soft hand. Suddenly his sex began to beat its wings. Philibert hunched over, his hands holding back the impatient bird. On her knees by Philibert, the lady dried his back, his chest, with motherly attention. Philibert wanted to hide his nakedness behind a wall. He grabbed the shower curtain, pulled it towards him and draped himself in it. The lady stepped back a few feet and looked at him with such tenderness that he felt something stinging behind his eyelids. He buried his head in the curtain. When he looked up again he saw the lady's hand gently opening her bodice, unbuttoning her dressing-gown all the way, then pulling it off first one shoulder then the other. The bathtub seemed as deep as the sea. At the sight of this woman's body Philibert knew he had nothing more to learn in life.

Between her perfumed, embroidered sheets, where she no longer looked like an old woman, sheets softer than her hands on his body, Philibert wept like a child without knowing why. And when the male strength

31

swelled his body to bursting, he let out a cry like a new-born baby.

Then he went out into the street without looking back. The air had that clear scent that he attributed to the woman of his dreams, before he knew that women sweat when they love.

*   *   *

It had snowed during the night. Why did he not notice when he first looked at her that the woman was so beautiful? He decided to go back and clean the walk in front of her house. She would see him, open the door for him and give him tea and buns and perhaps a little money. She had already given him some clothes, but unfortunately her miserly husband hadn't left anything in the pockets. The overcoat wasn't new but it looked as if it had been made for Philibert, who seemed to have his fortune made already. The lady was so rich. He would explain to her that he couldn't spend the rest of his life sleeping in churches, on a bench near the organ. His story would make her sad. No. She wouldn't understand a word of it, but she would invite him into her bed and they would laugh a lot as they ran around the house, her naked as Eve in Paradise, him wearing her husband's pyjamas. He would take his pipe today.

The city shouldn't have been called Montreal. It should have been called Bonheur. Happiness.

He grabbed a shovel that had been left in the snow near the sidewalk.

His shovel on his shoulder, he was happy, dancing as he went off in the direction of the sweet lady's house.

The streets ran right across the city, stretched out, crossed one another, made knots, formed letters that could only be deciphered from the sky, proliferated like jungle vines.

All at once a street had moved imperceptibly, another had twisted, trembling gently, and it seemed to Philibert that the immense hand of the city was closing up. He would be crushed between these streets that looked so much alike, with their names that all sounded the same and their uniform houses.

He had no idea where to find the house of the woman who had changed his life.

* * *

Their jackets open to the wind that bounced off the buildings, two soldiers were zigzagging along the sidewalk arm in arm, not upsetting anybody because everyone moved aside at the sight of them as though they were kings. The soldiers were yelling rather than singing, yelling a song Philibert wasn't familiar with. They burst out laughing between the words, laughing so hard they could hardly sing. Their words slurred into their laughter and their song was so funny they choked on it. The song was in English. "God Save the King," the soldiers stammered, but Philibert didn't understand. He thought he was listening to a bawdy song. It was time to learn some of those dirty songs and stories they still kept hidden from him in the village.

He followed the soldiers from a distance, but he was determined to hear them. He laughed, came up behind them, spied on them; he laughed with them and without realizing it he imitated the crazy stitchwork of their steps. Then, all at once, he had caught up with them.

"What do you want, little *Christ?*"

"I ain't no little *Christ,*" Philibert replied, "I'm a little *ciboire.*"

The two soldiers, rather taken aback, fell against a wall and laughed. They laughed, all hunched over, and spat and slapped their thighs to punctuate their delight. If they went on laughing Montreal would drown in their joyous saliva.

"What do you want?" one of the soldiers repeated, hiccuping.

"The war," said Philibert.

"When you got a face like a little girl that's never been screwed you don't go looking for no war!"

"The war, that's us! Yes sir!"

"If there ain't no *tabernacle* of a German in Montreal it's because Hitler's told them Lavigueur and Lafortune are in town."

One of the soldiers came closer to the boy to show him a mysterious object. A photograph.

"Hey, kid," he whispered, spitting. "Want to see Hitler's ass?"

"Sure," replied Philibert, suddenly envious of the soldiers.

"If you want to see his ass just look at his face. It's the same thing."

Staggering, the soldier called Lavigueur drew back a little in front of Philibert, then hurled himself forward. His big nailed boot was sticking out in front but Philibert dodged it and Lavigueur fell down in the snow with a splash. Lafortune, choked with laughter, stammered, "You ready to do a left right?"

"Yeah," he repeated, "are you ready to do a left right?"

Lavigueur got up then and stepped smartly onto the street, marching as though he were on the parade-ground, with steel bands in all his joints.

"Yes," said Philibert excitedly, "I'm ready to do a left right!"

Lavigueur and Lafortune hugged him and punched him. They had found a brother.

"Left! Right!"

Lavigueur gave the orders, Lafortune followed, and behind them, in triumph, Philibert went into a tavern, drunk before he had swallowed a drop.

He grimaced at the bitter taste of the first mouthful of beer, but how could he help but be carried away by the shouting and applause and the wild stamping of boots that acclaimed his first success at emptying a glass without putting it down for breath?

He drank.

He drank as much as the others.

He drank as long as his friends.

Glasses piled up along with the bottles that littered the table.

"Make some room," ordered Lavigueur.

Philibert cleared the table with the back of his hand and bottles and glasses shattered and crashed to the floor. But the uproar of broken glass was drowned in laughter.

They were drifting on a river of beer.

* * *

Suddenly Philibert saw people in front of him shivering in the slushy street. Pedestrians were spattered by mud splashed up by the cars. He was wearing a soldier's heavy jacket. Sticking his hands in the pockets he found cigarettes and a wallet.

"Those soldiers are going to come running after me, the *calvaires!* Just let them try and find me."

As fast as his wobbly legs could carry him Philibert took off. He thought he had been running for a long time when he read, in front of his eyes, in big red letters, FORUM. It couldn't be. He came closer to read it again, to check that the big red letters really spelled out that word. They did. It *was* the FORUM.

"*Baptême!* I'm going to see the Montreal Canadiens in flesh and skates!"

He ran up to the ticket-window. "I'll pay as much as you want but you have to give me a ticket. I want to see the Canadiens."

Inside, he ran up the steps. The crowd was on its feet, roaring and waving their arms. The ice was shining at the bottom of a vast pit. Above it, thousands of open mouths were sparkling, thousands of fists were raised in the air. There was an avalanche of shouts.

The players in their coloured sweaters carved the ice like flaming bolts of lightning. Despite the beer that was bubbling behind his eyes Philibert could read the numbers on the players' backs. And there it was! Number nine, the great Maurice Richard, the man with dynamite in his fists, the rocket-man who sped across the ice like a solitary bird in the vast blue sky.

"*Baptême!* It isn't true! It's real but it isn't true! *Hostie!* I can see Maurice Richard. It can't be! I don't see him!"

Maurice Richard crossed the blue line, then the red line, into the territory of the *maudits Anglais* from Toronto.

"Kill 'em!"

Philibert stood up.

"Kill 'em, Maurice!"

Richard reached the Toronto goal.

"Shoot! Shoot!"

"Come on Montreal, shoot!"

"Shut up, you fucking queer!"

"Shoot straight!"

Feet were fidgeting under the seats. Each foot imagined itself in one of Maurice Richard's skates. Philibert saw a laugh on Richard's face. It was like lightning that smiles before it strikes.

Far behind, the Toronto players were gasping for breath. Maurice Richard was happy. He tensed his fists inside his padded gloves and tensed his biceps under his sweater. Maurice Richard was getting ready to shoot. One of the Leafs came up behind him, stuck out his stick at one of Richard's legs, gave it a twist and Richard tripped. The *maudit Anglais* had hooked Maurice Richard! They couldn't take it when a little French Canadian like Richard was better than them.

Philibert, swearing with all his might, jumped over the boards and ran onto the ice. Not slipping but walking drunkenly, he slid towards the Toronto player, who had his back to him. There was a wall of broad padded shoulders in front of him. Philibert tapped his back. The Leaf turned his head and Philibert's fist landed in his teeth. The player wobbled foolishly, unable to locate the ice under his skates. He teetered and then fell full-length on the ice, crushed by the laughter all around him.

Philibert returned to his seat hastily, leaping over the boards. The crowd applauded, but he heard nothing. He felt friendly hands patting his back and ruffling his hair. He was surrounded by so much warmth and friendship that he wouldn't need to be liked by anyone else as long as he lived.

Because he was watching through tears, Maurice Richard was moving down below with unbearable awkwardness across the ice.

* * *

Philibert didn't find any more churches. All the temples in Montreal had been obliterated. They had fallen into the centre of the night.

Where would he sleep?

He followed streets as though they were his own footsteps through a forest where he would never again find his way.

Where had he slept the night before? He didn't remember, but his sleep had been soft. Tonight the darkness stuck thorns into his body.

* * *

Philibert was naked in a big room with red brick walls and no windows, with powerful lamps that gave off a dry light. He was standing up. The floor was so highly polished that he could see in it the reflection of his legs, the black stain that was his sex and his belly. Across from him, far away on the other side of the room, were men dressed in khaki, standing pressed close to one another, very rigid and so much alike they seemed not to have faces.

"He's pretty skinny," said a man dressed in white.

"His feet are as flat as fried eggs," said another man who looked just like the first one.

From the laughter that shook their caps Philibert could tell that the men in khaki had faces — all the same face.

An old soldier with a long white moustache came forward, his medals clinking against his chest. His steel-

tipped boots rang across the wooden floor. He ordered
Philibert to follow him. Philibert walked behind, infi-
nitely sad, up to the door of a cupboard where he had
hung — for ever he thought — the clothes that belonged
to the husband of the nice fat woman he loved.

* * *

An endless staircase clung to the wall, winding like
a demented plant in the rain. Philibert turned around
towards the bottom, then looked up towards the top. It
seemed as though he hadn't climbed a single step; the
staircase stretched on eternally and Philibert climbed it,
carrying the two cardboard boxes filled with clinking
jars of jam.

The steps seemed to be getting farther apart and
soon he would need another staircase between the steps,
there was so much space between them. "That *Christ* of
a staircase," Philibert complained. If Christ had had to
carry his cross up that staircase he never would have
made it to the end. "That *Christ* of a staircase . . ."
Christ would have thrown his cross down to the bottom
and it would have soared like a kite over the street. The
children would have shouted, "Look at the plane!" The
cross would have struck against a wall and rebounded
off another. "That *Christ* of a staircase . . ." The cross
would have gone sailing into a window and landed in a
bowl of soup or on top of a floury rump bouncing up
and down on a cackling housewife. "That *Christ* of a
staircase!"

Was Philibert to be condemned to carry cartons of groceries up a staircase for the rest of his life?

He threw the two cartons over the rail. With his arms free he raced down the staircase as though he were being pursued by flames. No hope of better future

*   *   *

The long snowy season was over. The sun in the sky was as red as the heart in the pictures of the Sacred Heart. Philibert was digging a trench down the middle of Sainte-Catherine Street. His pick and shovel were chewing painfully at the street. He broke through the asphalt covering, threw aside the crushed stone and the dead earth that smelled of oil. The heat of the asphalt burned his eyes and his arms and shoulders rubbed against the rough edges of the hardened earth under Sainte-Catherine Street. The asphalt gave off a bluish smoke, like oil; the street breathed slowly, like a sleeping belly. It would be a long day. The pick knocked off small chunks of earth that were as hard as the frozen ground in winter; but this was warm, this dead city earth. The hole gradually became a ditch and sometimes Philibert looked away, ahead of him. The gash in the street might close back up and Sainte-Catherine Street would come together like the Red Sea. It could swallow up Philibert, who was determined to dig a trench as wide as his shoulders. On either side of his head tires squealed, biting, with a smell of burning rubber. Philibert drew his head back. The wheel aimed at his face and Philibert

41

closed his eyes as he struck at the ground with his pick. The wheel went by without touching him, giving him only a mouthful of smoke that he spat out immediately. Sainte-Catherine Street is long and on either of Philibert's shoulders, bent around his shovel, tires screamed like circular saws. He turned his head aside abruptly, wheels passed by and returned, clattering like whips. Sainte-Catherine Street is long, and a pick is very slow in that earth turned into concrete.

Two well-polished boots sprang into sight. He didn't raise his eyes. A man was speaking to him. Philibert didn't understand the language but the man's words weighed on him, pushed at him. He speeded up his work with the pick until the polished boots had departed.

Sainte-Catherine Street is long. Philibert had never gone all the way to the end of it, but one day he would walk until it stopped somewhere. The ground was pitilessly hard. Philibert would be old when the ditch reached the end of Sainte-Catherine Street. If he never got to the end it would be because a wheel had crushed his head until it looked like a gutted cat lying in its own blood on the pavement, while his body would be stretched out at the bottom of the trench, ready to be buried. Philibert was digging his own grave down the middle of Sainte-Catherine Street.

It was true!

He knew it.

He threw his shovel under a truck that went roaring past.

He jumped out of the trench.

He ran across the street like a child. Without looking.

Then he disappeared into the city, far, far from Sainte-Catherine Street.

* * *

A brown wall pierced with windows as dark as the brick rose up before Philibert. Very high above his head pulleys were whining in their bearings. He pulled on a cable and his strength, multiplied by the pulley-block, raised the scaffold up into the wind. Was it the platform that was swaying, or the walls? He placed his hand on the brick. Everything stopped moving. The wall was upright, unmoving. He felt the steady weight of the wall in the brick, a tranquil strength.

Philibert's face was as dirty as his brush. He wanted to break the windows, punch a hole in the wall, let the cable slip through his hand, feel the burning of its fibres and then smash like an egg. But he was a man, wearing overalls, and condemned to clean away the black spittle of the Montreal sky.

He tied the cable firmly to make his scaffold fast. The sea of roofs beneath his feet was rough and dark.

An old bearded man had handed him a pamphlet that morning on Craig Street. He opened his overalls to pull it out of his pocket. The wind tried to take it away from him. Holding it tightly in his fingers Philibert read it through. "Men need a reason for living. Life is before us. At the very moment you are reading me, life should be beautiful."

"Life should be beautiful," Philibert repeated. "It's a *Christ* of a madman that wrote that."

He abandoned the printed sheets to the wind.

In front of him bricks were piled on top of bricks, cemented in the soot, extending in a wall from east to west, from ground to sky.

"Life should be beautiful."

Biting his lips Philibert attacked the brick as though he had claws instead of brushes in his hands.

"Life should be beautiful."

* * *

Machines for making the soles of shoes were chewing at the leather with loud cries. Then they were silent. The floor of the factory stopped vibrating and the workers tried to find their balance in the silence where their eardrums were ready to burst. Without speaking, they took paper bags from under their machines, opening them with caution as though they were afraid now that the sound of crumpling paper would be too loud. They didn't say a word. The knives that gnawed at the leather were still purring inside their ears, screaming insistently. And as he bit into his sandwich Philibert recalled what he had dreamed the night before.

"Hey you guys, want to hear what I dreamed last night? Even if it isn't dirty . . ."

The workers smiled, happy to hear a word above the mute machines; the dusty shadows disappeared from their faces.

"Old-timer," said Philibert to the one with white hair showing all around his greasy cap, "how long you been making boots? Since the war? You mean the first war, don't you? You never did nothing but make boots? And then the others came and they make boots too, and then me, I came and here I am making boots with the rest of you. We could go on making boots for the rest of our life. When we get to the Pearly Gates Saint Peter's going to ask us, What did you do with your lives? and we're going to answer, I made boots. If he's got any brains he'll tell us to go straight to hell, because it's one hell of a serious sin, spending your whole life making boots."

"What about your dream?" asked the old man.

"I always try to have dirty dreams," Philibert answered. "But this time I didn't make it. I dreamed I turned into a boot. Yeah, that's right, a boot. I was a boot and I was taking a stroll along Sainte-Catherine Street like a man. An ordinary boot. Believe it or not. I was a boot but I was thinking like a man. I was living like a man. On Saturday night when I went out to go dancing, instead of shaving my face I gave myself a nice shine. It's crazy. *Christ!* And when I went with a woman I was all nervous and I put myself away under the bed. When I got my pay-cheque I went to the bank. I went to work just like everybody else and I stood up in front of a machine for hours. You know what I did, me, the

45

boot? No? *Baptême,* I made boots! Then all of a sudden I started feeling uncomfortable. I felt my whole soul being squeezed like a foot in a boot that's too tight. I got sad. I didn't have the energy to get up in the morning. I came to my little square of space in the factory but I didn't go out dancing and I didn't go with women any more. I dragged my heel. I started to rot. I was sad. All of a sudden I heard somebody yelling, Hey, you down there, get to work. You don't get paid for daydreaming. I turned around. I was still a boot. I threw myself like a horseshoe and I landed right in the foreman's ass. I woke up right then. I wasn't a boot, I was a man. But I still smelled of leather.

"This morning when I was getting ready to come to the shop, standing in front of my mirror I couldn't look at myself without thinking that even if I looked like a man I was still a boot. *Hostie!* That's why I feel like booting somebody up the ass."

The old man blew his nose in his fingers.

"You want to boot somebody up the ass? Who?"

"The guy that's responsible," Philibert declared, as though it were perfectly obvious. "The guy that's responsible."

"The guy that's responsible," said the old man, "is the good Lord. He made the world the way he wanted, with rich guys and poor guys, with little guys like us and big guys."

Philibert gave the old man's lunch bag a kick that sent it flying into a pile of leather cuttings.

"The good Lord's like the boss. You don't get to see him too often. He doesn't hang around with people like us, the good Lord. Me, I'm getting out. I don't want to turn into a boot. Tell them to send me my pay."

The street didn't have its usual odour of damp leather and glue. It smelled good.

"Philibert!" somebody called.

He looked up. The old man was waving at him from a window. Philibert answered his friendly gesture and felt a sudden urge to go back to the factory, because of the old man. What was it about that smelly old man that made him want to go back to his prison?

"Philibert," said the old man, "if your father had brought you up properly you'd be a real diamond in the rough. You could be a Prime Minister."

"I'm not made out of stone, old-timer. I'm not stone, I'm . . . I'm . . ."

The words didn't come to him. He looked at the man with a cane on the other side of the street.

He walked off in the direction of the Gros Jambon Tavern.

He waited for the old man over his beer. He would have liked to drink with him. Then he didn't wait any longer. And he forgot him. Drunk, he was still drunk, so drunk he forgot his whole life.

When he woke up in his little room, he noticed a newspaper open on the floor near his bed. He didn't remember buying it. His aching head felt as though it were being split open with an axe. The news-print formed a grey mass, like a city seen from a distance, a

47

grey city in a black fog, untidy. Each little letter was a house attached to its neighbour, all of them knit together inextricably. It was a city, a real city. It was Montreal.

He heard the old man at the factory saying, "If your father had brought you up properly you'd have the makings of a Prime Minister."

Sorrow weighed on him, as heavy as a city.

* * *

Standing at the teller's wicket in the bank, Philibert felt as if his hands were paralysed. His fingers were unable to let go of the cheque that he held out to the cashier, his arm could not push his hand forward and his bones were too short or too long for his legs. He wanted to talk but the words turned thick, like molasses, on his lips. His shirt, soaked with sweat from work, smelled rotten under the arms and the filth from the shop was running down his forehead. He was dazzled by the beautiful eyes behind the grille. When the lips on the beautiful face parted gently in a smile, Philibert's lips came back to life at the same instant.

"Cash my cheque for me, gorgeous."

(He spoke loudly to give himself strength.)

"Do you wish to make a deposit, sir?"

"Maybe I do and maybe I don't."

The cashier was impatient.

"If you want to come to the Midway with me to see 'Tarzan and the Man-Eating Tigers' and go dancing afterwards, I won't make a deposit. But if you don't want to go out with me or if you're married you can put it all in the safe."

The cashier glanced professionally at the cheque, then she looked Philibert in the eye. "I'm through at seven."

Walking back to the bank all washed and shaved and perfumed, Philibert was so tall that the buildings drew back to let him pass. He contemplated the Savings Bank like a vegetable in his garden. The little cashier appeared in the revolving door, which at that hour of the day was being pushed frantically by people in a hurry. She was clutching her coat as though she were chilly. She passed in front of the dazed Philibert without seeing him. Then she jumped into a car that went roaring off with its door still open.

"Christ on a bun with onions!"

The car roared impatiently at a red light.

"Taxi!"

A taxi pulled up to the curb.

"Catch up with that yellow Pontiac."

He pulled a two-dollar bill out of his pocket.

"Hold on. This'll give you some speed."

The car shot ahead and Philibert sank back into the seat. Cars were coming from all sides. The taxi wove among the blinding headlights and caught up with the yellow Pontiac.

"What do we do now?"

"Follow them."

The two cars swallowed up streets, jumped across intersections. Red lights twinkled as the two cars sought and fled each other like lost lovers. They made unexpected detours. They squealed and growled like savage animals, weaving in and out of traffic, their wheels clawing at the highway, the bodies seemingly on fire.

The pavement was in an uproar. The two vehicles howled, the yellow Pontiac and the taxi. They barked and hurled insults at each other. They moved along towards the yellow spring that was the sun until the Pontiac seemed to sink into it.

"Stop!" Philibert yelled. "Stop!" he repeated, pounding on the taxi-driver's back.

As he braked the car the road moaned and there was a smell of scorched flesh.

"Stop! Are you deaf? I don't want to get myself wiped out here!"

With difficulty, the taxi reined in. Before it had come to a complete stop Philibert turned his pockets inside out to empty them of money.

"I'm getting out of here."

He jumped out of the car, which was still moving, squealing along the pavement. Ahead of him the Laurentians looked like the muscular arms of men. It was almost winter.

He had to go back to Montreal, back to his new room. Perhaps the landlord had replaced the cardboard in the broken window-panes with glass. Philibert turned his back on the mountain.

Cars punched holes in the air around him.

He leaned against a fence. Cars swam through the night like luminous fish. He wouldn't be happy until he owned a yellow Pontiac.

Philibert saw himself in his long yellow Pontiac, pushing the chrome-plated buttons, the ground rolling by under him at whatever speed he commanded.

* * *

He tore open the envelope with trembling hands.

How could the letter have come all the way here to this room where the water-pipes rumbled like a hungry belly?

His letter quivered before his eyes like the flame of a little lamp in the window of his childhood. He was sorry that his childhood was so far away. He was sorry that he was so far away. Life back there was waiting for him with the fragrance of fresh bread. Tears came to his eyes. It was too sad, the life of the people he had left behind. It was like a quiet nightmare. Montreal weighed on his shoulders like a stone, but he was free. He was free, but the people in the village were crushed beneath their sky. Through his tears Philibert read the words that had the shape of what he knew best, his village. "My dear boy . . ." (Was it his mother's hand that had trembled? Or was it his own hand, with its black finger-nails, clutching the letter?)

"Did you hear in Montreal that your Uncle Fabien got himself ruined by some Montreal robbers, three of them and they only talked English, they said their

51

names but it wasn't their real names so we don't even know who it was that ruined your uncle and he told me that he hasn't seen you for a long time and he'd love to see you and he said you must be a real gentleman by now with a moustache but I said to Fabien Philibert's still young, he's got to earn his living, he won't forget us, he'll come and see us when he can. Your Uncle Fabien had to mortage his land that was all paid for for the simple reason that our late father, your grandfather had sold it to him for ninety-nine cents cash on one condition only that the daughter-in-law, Fabien's wife, had to take care of the old man and our late father couldn't get out of his bed to eat before he died and he used to spill his pea soup on the sheets so the daughter-in-law used to insult poor Fabien till our poor father died and Fabien was working on the land since he was twelve and if any oats grew up in between the rocks it was from Fabien's sweat and because the priest came and blessed his fields with holy water every summer because God's blessing works very well for oats and also anything else a man decides to do, so anyway you could say that Fabien's land belonged to him and even if he was our father's favourite he didn't steal that land because if you ask me he took just as good care of it as our late father. That was his land, Fabien, maybe you remember or maybe you don't but anyway he never said my land's going to give so much oats, he said I'm going to give so much oats and he never said my cow had a calf but I had a calf and he wasn't wrong either. But anyway Fabien lost that land of his. Poor Fabien, it isn't his any more because he mortaged himself. On the train to Quebec City, the long one that goes through Valley Junction, he met these three *Anglais* that didn't speak a word of French and they were going to come and build a factory right here in our village. So Fabien mortaged his land and signed a cheque for five thousand three hundred and fifty-two dollars and each one of the three *Anglais* signed one too just like it, they'd been drinking in the train a little but when you're on a trip you're on a trip. So anyway two weeks later the three *Anglais* came to give him a diploma that said he was a vice-president, not the same vice that's in the catechism, but anyway Fabien was going to have a job at the factory he wasn't over the *Anglais* but he was just as important and he had this diploma that had official signatures on it but you couldn't read them. So Fabien managed to sell them the wood they needed for their building and the *Anglais* accepted because he made them a little refund, you can't get something for nothing, and these big trucks came from Montreal, great big red ones if you ever see any, but the *Anglais* weren't driving them it was French Canadians like us and they took the wood in their trucks that looked as if they were going to collapse and Fabien hasn't got his Ford any more and he had to pay for his land just as if our late father hadn't already paid for it so anyway he wanted to get a lawyer to defend him and so he had to mortage his cows and the lawyer sold the cows and afterwards he said the *Anglais* had acted within the law and you couldn't do anything against the law and poor Fabien said the only thing he had left that wasn't mortaged was his dink and at his age . . . So you see you shouldn't get carried away with ambition. Have you got a cold or the piles?

"Your mother who doesn't forget you and who you don't forget and who prays to the good Lord for you."

Philibert could read no more because of the tears that were veiling his eyes.

He opened the vent in the window part way and dropped the little bits of the torn-up letter down among the kleenexes that blew in the wind.

*   *   *

The scraps of the letter fluttered and fell for so long that it seemed there was no ground to stop their fall.

In order not to be sad, Philibert had forgotten. He had forgotten, as a traveller gradually abandons his baggage in order to make the route less painful. He did not want his eyelids weighed down with tears that would never flow.

Because he refused to be sad Philibert covered his father in an oblivion that was heavier than the damp earth. He forgot his mother because he did not want to encounter his memories of her at the corner of the street, nor see her face reflected in a window or in the sooty bricks. How could he think of his mother without being too sad to go on living? How could he think of his mother, that frail young girl who didn't dare to smile in the old photograph in the album? How could Philibert keep from weeping at the memory of that young girl he had never known? The beauty had been destroyed by her children as by voracious ants. The children had nested in her belly, distended it and made her breasts sag, swelled the legs that Philibert had glimpsed dark beneath her long skirts. Nights without sleep had taken the colour from her face and the children who had died drifted in the murky water of her eyes. Her fourteen children continued to cling to her breast as though they had never been severed from it.

When Philibert held a young girl's body in his arms he was afraid to break the thin mirror that reflected his joy. A fat old woman might spring out of it.

* * *

Before he went to work Philibert gulped down a sandwich. His newspaper was open at the financial section. What was the meaning of the long columns of figures, all the fractions and letters running down the page? It was written in French but for all he understood it might as well have been Polish.

"When I think about all the things I don't know . . ."

Someone scratched at his door. Philibert recognized his landlord's manner. The little man with red hair beckoned to Philibert. His wife was waiting for him in the hallway, wearing a black dress as she always did, but today her dress hung to her heels.

"We've found out a lot of things," the obsequious little man whispered.

"So we've decided it's time to teach you some too," the little woman went on.

"Come . . ."

The little man opened a door, the one to the most peaceful room on the ground floor. Philibert thought no one lived in it. The doorway was veiled by a heavy black curtain that the little man raised with a religious hand. Philibert hesitated. What did they want of him? The woman gave him a motherly push. The black curtain smelled like a church. Philibert moved it aside and entered the room. One candle shed a meagre light in the black room. The door closed again. The lock clicked. The woman replaced the curtain. She and the man each took one of Philibert's arms and led him to the flickering candle. There was not enough light to see, but Philibert suspected that the walls were covered with black draperies. They came to a table, covered with a black cloth on which the candle had been placed. Near the candle there was a black shape. A box.

"Now," the little man whispered, "you are going to become a man."

"Now," said the woman, "you are going to learn the only thing a man needs to know."

Because he was uneasy Philibert teased them.

"There's only one thing a man's got to know and lots of girls have showed me before now."

The little man clapped his hand over Philibert's mouth.

"Don't blaspheme on the day of your birth."

He took his hand away and turned towards the candle.

"Come."

His hands, lit by the yellow flame, lifted the cover of the black box. The woman held the flame over it. Philibert started as though a bat had brushed his face with its wings. In the mixture of light and shadow he could see, lying in the box, a little white skeleton with minuscule bones.

"What's that?" he asked, restraining a shriek.

"That is life," said the little man.

"That is life," echoed his wife.

"We do not die."

"We do not die."

The little man replaced the cover, tenderly.

"Kneel," he ordered.

Philibert had no intention of disobeying. The man went to the other side of the table and stood across from Philibert. With a look of infinite hardness, a hardness that Philibert did not know he possessed, the man spread his arms and cried, in a voice that seemed to want to tear the city apart, "We do not die. We do not die. We do not die. The body that is placed in the earth is a seed of life. We do not die. We do not die. The seed germinates and another life comes out of it, a human being who is purified of life. We do not die. We do not die. To die is to live. To live. Our child lives!"

Philibert's knees were riveted to the floor. He lacked the strength to get up and leave, to spit out the disgust that was welling in his throat. He heard his tight-pressed lips repeat, "To die is to live."

* * *

"Goddamn *papier!*"

"It's a *journal,* boss; not a *papier.* It's *Montréal-Matin.*"

"Throw away that goddamn paper! *Travaille.* Money."

Big Papatakos, shouting, yanked the newspaper out of Philibert's hands. His fingers, stained brown from garlic and tobacco, made dollar-counting gestures under Philibert's nose.

"Money! Work! That's the life!"

The big hand pushed Philibert down to the cellar. Papatakos had taken away the electric lights, and it was like night down there, as dark as the time before Creation. Electricity isn't cheap.

The Greek had told Philibert, "It's a job you can do with your eyes shut."

So the young man acquiesced to show that he had lots of experience in this kind of work.

"If you can do it with your eyes shut I guess you don't need any lights."

Philibert was condemned to peel potatoes in total darkness. When he went upstairs for his meal the light, made cloudy by the greasy window of the *Chez Papa* Restaurant, scratched his eyes.

Sometimes a burst of laughter would leap at his face like a rat. Rats. He had heard them nibbling along one of the walls, their claws digging into the wood of the boxes that had been abandoned along with their rotting contents. Sometimes he heard them rummaging among the sacks of potatoes. The laughter came from the back of the cellar, from the other side of a wall that his eyes, grown used to the night, could make out in the solid shadow.

On the other side, a woman was laughing. She laughed often, harshly, as though she were a little bit afraid, a little bit amused, he thought. Each time, he gave a start. And now, as her laughter tore the cellar night, Philibert threw a potato at the wall. The projectile bounced back and there was no reply. Philibert went on with his work. The clammy potato peelings wound around his wrist and the potato slipped between his fingers. To forget, he started to think about what he had read in the newspaper.

The Government had built a bridge in a flat pasture where there was neither a river nor a stream. There was no road leading to the bridge; there wasn't even a road to the pasture. The Minister who had ordered it to be built had told the reporters, "Our party has given you a bridge; you can trust us. Soon we'll give you a river to go under it, to say nothing of a road that will lead directly to this magnificent bridge, built on the model of the most modern bridges in America. It's clear proof that our little French Canadians can be the geniuses of modern technology. Here's what we're going to do. We'll put boats on the river if you like. Our party wants to guarantee that there's work for the French Canadians in Québec. Without taking anything away from the *Anglais,* of course, who are at home here too. We will not tolerate having French Canadians condemned to unemployment here in *la belle province.* We'll build bridges where we want them. That's our absolute, our inalienable right under the Constitution of 1867. Our party builds and creates jobs — thousands of jobs, 100,000 jobs — while the Opposition weeps and moans and claims it isn't a good idea to give work to the heads of good honest Catholic families. No, the Opposition will never stop us from building our bridges. There are two kinds of people who disapprove of this bridge: the Opposition and the Communists. Are you with us or with them?"

Philibert tossed a potato in the air: the Minister's brain. But perhaps he was very intelligent?

Philibert had read another article, hidden away on the page with the birth and death announcements. "Plain Talk from a Psychologist to the People of Québec." Philibert could see the short article as clearly as though he had the printed page before his eyes. "Following investigations and in-depth studies we can now say with certainty that the chief obstacle for the young man from the lower strata of society is his fascination with failure. The young man from these strata of society prefers failure to success. He devotes his whole life to preparing for his failure. This young man has only one basic desire: to punish himself for his deprived childhood. A lifetime of failure, following a modicum of success, is a fair punishment for him, according to statistics from the Michigan Institute of Psychology. In conclusion, we would say that the young man from modest surroundings should be informed of this danger, and quickly. As he travels the road of life the young man must ask himself, Am I preparing for success or for failure?"

In the cellar of the *Chez Papa* Restaurant, in the rotten night that recalled to Philibert the muddy earth his father dug in the spring, he repeated, "Am I preparing for failure?"

Then all the streets of Montreal were leading him to failure. When he had travelled all the roads that lay in wait for him and all the streets that appeared before him, Philibert would drop from exhaustion and he would have to say, "It was all useless." He carried the embryo of failure inside him. It was growing and it would feed on him until it devoured him from within. One day when it was big enough the embryo would tear Philibert apart; it would get out and fall on him, it would crush him like a rock.

There in the night Philibert hurled his knife and heard it sink into the wall. He ran up the stairs into the restaurant as though a dog were after him. He pushed the door and ran right into Papatakos whose greenish face had been invaded by fat smiling jowls.

61

"*Argent.* Money. It's payday. Here's your money."

The Greek pulled a little bundle of bills, folded in four, out of the pocket of his shirt and held them in his fat fingers, which looked like the pickles on display in his front window. But he didn't give them to Philibert.

"What will you do with all this money? You want to go direct to Heaven?"

The big cheeks, spluttering, came close to Philibert's ear. The whispers changed to little snickers that must have made the cockroaches jump. Philibert laughed a little. Papatakos had moved back to wait for his answer. He gave in. Then Papatakos put his arm around Philibert's shoulder affectionately while with his big hand he replaced the little packet of dollars that Philibert had earned in the pocket of his greasy shirt.

Papatakos led Philibert to a door marked "Out of bounds — Administration." He opened the door and gave Philibert a fatherly push. Philibert's heart beat like the wings of a bird on its way to Heaven, but his feet trembled as they sought the first step leading to the cellar, which was not completely dark. The last step disappeared into a damp curtain that smelled of tobacco. Behind it, he could make out a lighted lamp.

"Come in," said a woman, indifferent.

Philibert pushed aside the curtain which slid along a horizontal track. A woman was stretched out on a bed, wearing a bathrobe. She didn't take her eyes from her magazine to look at him.

"Take off your clothes," the woman ordered, her lips moving around a cigarette.

To show her that he wasn't trembling as he looked at her, and that she wasn't the first woman he had seen in a bed, Philibert undid his fly. But he knew that the woman could guess, as each button slipped through the buttonhole, that a sad clock was striking inside him. His pants dropped to the floor. The woman put down her cigarette without extinguishing it, put her magazine by the pillow and took off her bathrobe. Lying down again, she picked up her magazine and her cigarette.

As he climbed the stairs he felt as if his body had been flayed. He was sad. When the woman was in his arms he had wept because he felt so little joy. He was hungry. He'd given Papatakos his week's wages so he could go to Heaven. But where would he go for a meal?

The Greek saw him come up from the cellar and a greenish smile spread over his coarse features.

"I'm going to peel you some potatoes," said Philibert. "Can I get my pay right away?"

"Go on, go on, young man. Time is money."

There was a grease-spattered photograph hanging near the door to the cellar. Philibert had looked at it many times as he passed. It was a picture taken at Papatakos' wedding. The inane smiles radiated joy under the gummy glass. This time though, the picture held Philibert's attention. He couldn't take his eyes off it. The woman on Papatakos' arm, younger but quite recognizable, was the one Philibert had just left in the bed in the cellar.

The cellar's mouldy breath did not relieve Philibert's heart. He found his potatoes. The knife made a damp little sound under the peel that slid around his wrist like a long worm.

In this cellar, under the beams, the night seemed like coarse black earth, stinking and heavy, that had been poured over Philibert.

Perhaps it was sunny outside in the city, with people coming and going, hurrying and loitering, thousands of feet passing over his head. Life was not for him. He was buried while others enjoyed themselves.

On the other side of the night, from behind the partition, a coarse laugh exploded. The woman hadn't laughed when she was with Philibert. Why was she laughing now? He grabbed a handful of potatoes and bombarded a wall with them. He threw his knife somewhere, shot up the stairs, pushed the door as though he wanted to tear it off its hinges and went up to Papatakos. Placing his feet firmly on the floor, puffing out his chest, he announced, "I'm getting out."

Papatakos didn't understand. He grimaced, but he didn't laugh. He wiped his hands on his shirt, glistening with oil.

"Papa . . . takos," said Philibert, "I'm going because when I look at you I don't know if it's your face I see or your wife's rear end."

Outside, he spat in the face of spring.

*   *   *

Philibert sold his watch so he could eat that night. He picked at a cold ham omelette that didn't taste very good. He didn't like ham and he didn't like eggs. His fork gave up and clinked against the empty beer bottles in front of him. He talked. He was alone in a corner where the yellow light of the Leonardo da Vinci Pizza Hot Dog turned grey.

"Can anybody prove to me that I was put on this earth just to peel potatoes for Papatakos? It isn't fair. If there was any justice everybody would have to peel potatoes. But then there'd be too many people in the cellar. If you're looking for real justice, everything fair, you'd have to look in Heaven. But you can't find Heaven. It doesn't exist, no more than I've got tits. Papatakos' wife's got nice big tits but that doesn't mean there's a Heaven."

Three faces near his table were listening to him with religious attention, as though his voice were the voice of their own thoughts.

"The *Anglais* made the war because they had factories. They built tanks and machine-guns and rifles. Then they shit gold turds like the priest's servant's holy dog. The French Canadians didn't want the war though. Oh no, they were scared of the war like they're scared of the devil, *hostie*. They didn't have any factories, the French Canadians. No weapons to sell, no boots, no cannons. They didn't want the war because they were afraid they'd lose their arms and their legs and the thing they use to plough their wives. Some day the French Canadians are going to have their own factories and when they do they'll make war on the *maudits Anglais* to make the wheels turn in those factories. And when

65

there isn't a single *maudit Anglais* left the French Canadians will make wars with each other. And then the French Canadians will shit gold nuggets too, *hostie!*"

He emptied another glass.

"I would've liked to go to the war, to get away from things, jump over the wall. I didn't ask to be born. It's like a kick in the ass. I've been wondering why ever since."

Philibert was silent. The beating of his heart resounded in his temples but it was beating for nothing; his hands were calloused from all the painful jobs they had done, for nothing. He breathed for nothing, he had been born for nothing, he got drunk for nothing. And it was for nothing that he had left his village where people died for nothing like dry trees. Those people made children for nothing, and they had spent their lives in fear and poverty for nothing. The long road that had brought Philibert to Montreal had led him to nothing. And it was for nothing that he came back to his miserable little room every evening, the bitter taste of the day's work in his mouth. It was a taste that made him want to vomit as though he had wiped the filthy streets of Montreal with his tongue.

"You live. Then all of a sudden you're dead. If you're rich your soul rots like an old potato. If you're poor you get wiped out by a bus or maybe a truck . . . squashed like a flea. Ah, Christ! What did I want to say? Doesn't matter. Whether I talk or shut up the world's going to stay under my feet and the moon's going to stay up there like an *hostie* of a nun's fat white ass."

*   *   *

Philibert was on his knees on the floor of the Leonardo da Vinci Pizza Hot Dog. His pants were wet from the soapy water on the linoleum and his hand had gone to sleep as he pushed the slimy rag back and forth. His shadow followed his motions without becoming completely indistinguishable from the grey linoleum.

Behind the drawn curtains, by the miserable light of the one lamp the Italian allowed him to leave on, Philibert tried to picture women's faces, but it seemed as if the wet rag had wiped out their images too. Philibert's hand wandered under the tables, slid between the legs, under the benches. He murmured names, but the names refused to assume their fleshly forms in this night of his memory. Philibert was alone. He was sad to be so alone and proud to be so sad. In this way he could insult life. Nobody loved him; that didn't wipe him out. Animals in the field don't love each other, why should men?

When he had picked up the cigarette butts and wiped up all the mud and stains, Philibert replaced the chairs; then, folding the newspaper he always carried in his pocket, he sat down in the boss's place in front of the cash-drawer. He lit a cigarette and while the city slept he read how very simple things become inextricably tangled up.

People would go on dying and being born. People had no desire to cure their evil nature.

* * *

TANCREDE PAPINEAU

The name was printed in big red letters. Philibert had never seen it or heard it before. Tancrède Papineau's face looked insignificant on the enormous poster: a lump of whitish clay that had not been modelled by life. Smooth hair, vacant eyes, thin moustache. "The Man of the Future," according to the poster.

About twenty people were standing in front of the picture, waiting, smoking, stamping their feet. They spoke little. Like Philibert, they were there because of a small advertisement in *Montréal-Matin.*

A pot-bellied man with tiny hands appeared, fiery as a general.

"You realize that the people are going to elect their leaders tomorrow."

He waved an accusing fist towards Tancrède Papineau's poster. Then he jumped up, ripped it off the wall and tore it furiously to shreds.

"Tancrède, we're going to put you through the meat-grinder. Any questions?"

A few impatient coughs. They had come for a job, not to ask questions.

"Go to room 129. They'll give you some bags with pictures of Tancrède in them. They have to be distributed. All over."

"How much do we get paid?" asked a man with a pipe.

"Honestly. We'll count your empty bags. No cheating, now. You have to distribute the pictures one by one, from door to door. Don't stick them in the garbage can. You'll be watched."

"Do we get paid some week with four Thursdays, or today?" asked Philibert.

"Come to the Midnight Café at five o'clock. You'll be paid in cash. And there'll be some women for the men that don't turn up their noses at things like that. Women from the Party."

Like his companions who were going to distribute papers through the neighbourhood, Philibert hung a bag over each shoulder and set off at a run. He got winded climbing stairs, zigzagged through the streets from one house to another, sticking photographs in letter slots and under doors. Then on to another street. His bags were empty. A car was following him with more bags waiting in the trunk. At the wheel, an eye was observing.

A few hours later every voter had seen the photograph. They laughed. They were scandalized. They were disappointed. Or disgusted.

The photograph showed Tancrède Papineau, naked behind his glasses, in the bed of a young television actress. On the back, Josette Latendresse had written: "Vote for my Tancrède. He knows what to do."

Now no one, assuredly, would vote for the infamous Papineau, that hypocrite, sinner and sex maniac.

The photographs drifted along the streets and into the schoolyards where they had been sent by the wind. Young boys picked them up, laughing lewdly.

Philibert went back to his room. He was happy because he had been paid.

He would not be voting tomorrow.

"My X on a piece of paper isn't going to change the world. It'll turn whichever way it wants to."

* * *

Philibert pressed the grease-smeared bell-button.

The door, as it opened, tore through the rancid shadow. He found himself facing a mountain. At the peak, in a cloud of black beard, was a face.

"I . . . I . . . I . . . read your ad in . . . *La Presse.*"

"Knock me!" thundered the mountain.

Philibert thought he had misunderstood. The mountain repeated, in strangely-accented French this time, "Hit!"

The mountain got to its knees, the big head coming down to Philibert's level. The breath that came out of it stank like the exhaust fumes of a garbage truck.

"Hit me!"

The bristly hair and beard did not completely conceal the face, stained with blue scars.

"Are you afraid of to hit me?"

Philibert's fist struck at a rock of flesh. He ran to the staircase, afraid of being bashed into crumbs himself. The mountain rolled over behind him. He felt the vast breath in his back, its bitter warmth. Something seized him by the shoulder.

"You know to drive automobile?"

"Yes."

"You are brave. You are now private chauffeur of Boris Rataploffsky, the Ninth Vonder of Vorld."

* * *

Glowing with pride, the private chauffeur of the Ninth Wonder of the World sat behind the steering wheel of which he would henceforth be in charge. The cab of the truck would not contain his enormous boss; the giant travelled in the back, in a made-to-measure cabin. He had had a plywood box built on the chassis of the truck, the windows in the sides decorated with curtains made heavy by dirt. His throne was composed of two armchairs he had put together, nailed and sewed. The cabin was painted red with big white letters reading, "The Man with the Face of Steel"; smaller letters read, "Boris Rataploffsky"; and in bigger letters, "The Ninth Wonder of the World."

How could Philibert not be proud? The eyes of all Montreal were on his truck. People stopped and turned around to see it drive by. Cars slowed down, braked suddenly and risked collisions to have a look at the truck carrying the Ninth Wonder of the World. It was the first time in his life that Philibert had felt proud.

71

A small bell rang behind his head. Boris Rataploffsky had given the signal. The truck stopped across from the *Comme Chez Vous* Tavern and Philibert ran to the back to open the doors. The Man with the Face of Steel got out with all the majesty of God the moment after Creation. When the huge foot touched the ground Montreal seemed to sink a little.

Boris Rataploffsky, preceded by Philibert, walked through the tavern. His big belly pitched and heaved above the tables and overturned chairs.

"Set us up!" Philibert ordered, surprised by his own authority.

The old waiter conscientiously brought several trays filled with glasses of beer and arranged them so that they covered the table. Around Philibert and the giant the most animated conversations fell silent.

Boris Rataploffsky, his little finger raised, drank glass after glass, row after row, very carefully, without spilling a drop of beer. He emptied them as though he were inhaling a whiff of air. No one else dared to drink. Life had come to a halt in the *Comme Chez Vous* Tavern. The giant's table was covered with empty glasses where the foam traced fine embroideries.

"Go on, my boy," said the giant.

Philibert adjusted his cap and stood up. "Ladies and gentlemen, mesdames et messieurs. You see before you the one, the only, the brilliant Boris Rataploffsky, the Man with the Face of Steel, the Ninth Wonder of the World, the Queen of England's favourite athlete. He gets a pension from the King of Brazil and the King of

Hungary refused to pass over to the other side without seeing Boris Rataploffsky."

The giant coughed. When he was impatient, he coughed. Philibert hurried on.

"Your punches are like flea farts to this giant. Mesdames et messieurs, don't miss this chance to hit a giant. For one dollar you can hit him in the eye or on the mouth. Fifty cents and you can try for his nose and for a quarter you get to hit him anywhere else on the face. Careful! Don't get hurt! Step right up! Pay here. We won't be back. Hit the giant! Pansies, call for your mummies!"

In the cushions of his flesh, Boris Rataploffsky was dreaming.

"Come on, come on! Ladies and gentlemen! The giant won't hurt you. His steel face feels no pain."

A customer came up, taking off his jacket.

"I'm going to wake up that big *ciboire* of a pile of dead meat."

The brave man paid his dollar and, proudly rolling up his sleeves, he walked up to face the Man with the Face of Steel. He caressed his fist with his other hand, stamping like a horse about to kick. He straightened out his fist, clenched it again, tightened it, made it hard and sharp with all his might. All at once he hit the giant. The frightened customer was already far away. The giant slept on.

Philibert's hand was filled with bills and fists fell in an avalanche on the unfeeling mountain. Nothing disturbed the shadows of the face.

The customers hit until they had exhausted themselves. They had less and less strength. They laughed. The giant's thoughts were elsewhere.

Suddenly a little drop of blood was visible in his eyebrow.

"*Baptême!*" Philibert panicked. "It isn't true he's got a face of steel."

He yelled, gesturing broadly, "OK, that's it. All over now."

The Ninth Wonder of the World left the tavern behind Philibert, whose pockets were heavy with the money they had accumulated. Without a word he got into his cabin in the red truck with the flat springs.

Philibert put the take into his outstretched hands. A smile flickered in the beard. Philibert closed the door of the cabin.

* * *

Philibert broke a dozen eggs, sliced a salami, added onions, red and green peppers and cream, mixed it all up in a saucepan with his hands and then cooked it on the gas-stove, which was no longer sticky since he had cleaned it.

The Ninth Wonder of the World ate the omelette with the enthusiasm of a child. Philibert would never get used to his strength. When the Man with the Face of Steel spoke, Philibert shuddered as the house of his childhood had shuddered in the wind.

"Monsieur Rataploffsky, I've got an idea."

"An idea? Show me it."

Philibert explained: it was a mistake for the Ninth Wonder of the World to display himself in half-empty taverns and miserable restaurants where the neighbours got together for a smoke. Only the great arenas were worthy of an attraction as spectacular as the Man with the Face of Steel. Instead of putting on his show several times a day, Boris Rataploffsky could make more money by exhibiting himself in the big arenas, before delirious crowds.

The giant applauded.

"You're my man. You'll be my manacher."

"OK. And from now on my name is Phil. Monsieur Phil. Mister Phil. Manager! *Baptême*! I can't believe myself."

* * *

From spring until fall the red truck took the Ninth Wonder of the World from Montreal to Gaspé, from Rouyn to Sherbrooke. Everywhere he was given a royal welcome. On his manager's advice, he wore a gold cape with "The Man with the Face of Steel" embroidered on it. In the cities he was surrounded by children and pimply-faced adolescents and old men. They were all the same age before Boris Rataploffsky, as they pushed and jostled, marvelled and bickered, trying to get a chance to touch the Ninth Wonder of the World. They were ecstatic, doubtful; they argued. If the giant raised his hand they stepped back.

Phil always walked ahead of his boss. He busied himself pretending to chase away the importunate. He told them on every possible occasion that just the night before he had refused to sell the giant for the sum of three thousand dollars to American interests. "We already sold too many of our natural resources to foreigners," he would conclude.

All along the highways linking the arenas, through the poor, interminable forests or the flat infinite plains, the giant sang. Phil didn't understand the words of his strange songs that made the roof of his cabin quiver, but he sensed that they were words of joy.

*   *   *

In the middle of the ring, whose ropes had been painted white for the occasion, the Man with the Face of Steel stood motionless under the bombardment of fists. The volcano was sleeping.

"Step right up!" shouted Phil over the loud-speakers. "Here's your chance to hit a bigger man than you are. Right this way!"

All around the ring there were children, pallid labourers, muscular lumberjacks, coughing schoolboys, salesmen with slicked-down hair and distinguished ladies; they grew impatient or startled or placed bets. They climbed into the ring, saluted the crowd, and hit. Joyous applause. Each blow was greeted by a delighted ouburst from the crowd. They paid and began all over again, twice, three times. Their pleasure grew. The distinguished ladies kept their rings on their fierce little hands.

At times a stain would appear on the eyelid of the Face of Steel. An old wound reopening or a badly-healed scab. A little blood would flow. Then the fists would let loose, attacking the Face of Steel on all sides, hitting as though you had to destroy to live, as if the giant's face were a prison wall. Their strength increased with each blow. The giant coughed slightly and the fists persisted as though they were attacking a vanquished fawn.

There were shouts of joy and dancing in the shaking stands. Phil could not pick up all the bills that flew around his head like crazy birds. He was powerless to control the crowd. Like a nation of ants they swarmed into the ring, ready to assault the too kindly giant. There were ten of them hitting without let-up, and without paying.

Phil shouted, "Pay right here! Pay here! It's cheap!"

Suddenly the Ninth Wonder of the World stood up, yelling as though he were spitting fire. Before the shock-waves struck the walls he picked up a big man and threw him among the spectators, where he was crushed like an egg. The giant had already grabbed three other men; these he threw at the ceiling. When the three unfortunates had dropped to the floor the angry mountain fell on them with the force of a landslide.

The crowd was silent.

Women wept.

Lovers let their arms fall from their girlfriends' waists.

The giant came up to Phil, putting a hand as heavy as an ox on the boy's shoulder. Blood was streaming from his mouth.

"You are good boy," he grunted. "Don't forget."

Big tears mingled with his blood.

The Man with the Face of Steel climbed out of the ring and went towards one of the exits. He knocked over everything in his path, crushing it like grass.

The bleachers were on the edge of a gentle lake. The giant walked along the shore and got into a rowboat that sank almost out of sight under the burden of his enormous weight.

Phil called, "Wait for me!"

The giant didn't listen. He rowed, but the submerged boat moved along painfully, an island adrift. The giant put the oars inside the boat. Gently, it came to a stop.

Then very slowly the Ninth Wonder of the World got up and let himself fall into the water. He didn't try to swim. He was no longer a giant but a man.

His body was found by a child swimming in the last rays of the sun.

"Who was Boris Rataploffsky?"

"What country did he come from?"

Phil didn't know. He was too drunk, they said. Phil assured them that he knew nothing of the giant's life.

He replied, "What's the use of being a giant on the earth? What's the use of being an ordinary man?"

They laughed.

Sitting in the water that lapped at the sand, Philibert wept.

*   *   *

Real life, the life that set Phil's blood on fire, crackled in the nightclubs on Saint-Laurent Boulevard. His laughter was already famous there, as well as the enthusiastic way he applauded the dancing-girls.

When they left the stage they moved among the customers on the way to their dressing-rooms. Anita the African Tigress ran her claws through Phil's hair. Her caress enflamed him as though he had had too much to drink. He had money in the inside pockets of his jacket, a ring on every finger and alligator shoes. Walking proudly, he followed the fiery serpent that disappeared into her dazzling sequins.

Phil wanted Montreal to clasp him and stifle and drown him. He wanted to be a brick among the other bricks, but alive. He wanted to live.

He liked the warm sidewalks in the slums that gave off an aroma of hot dogs and sausages with onions. He liked the life hidden behind the windows papered with photographs of girls. And he liked the life circulating in the buildings' concrete façades that were closed like impenetrable faces.

In the room with flowered wall-paper, beneath a framed picture of Our Lady, the heart pierced with the Seven Sorrows, Phil sweated, exhausted and out of breath from his efforts to transmit the fire that was in him. The girl under him was a soft living corpse.

He got up, running his fingers through his hair. He rummaged in the pockets of his jacket and pulled out a piece of paper, unfolding it carefully. It was a poster that he held out to the African Tigress. A pout. She was disappointed that it wasn't money. She grimaced at the big photograph of The Man with the Face of Steel.

"It's an ape!"

"Read," he ordered proudly.

He pointed: Mr. Phil, Manager.

He pulled on his clothes, picked up the poster the girl had dropped to the floor and refolded it carefully.

He left Saint-Laurent, wanting to vomit.

Farther away, Montreal looked like a funeral wreath placed on the ground.

* * *

In the smoky room the night was already brightening.

Phil spoke as though he were reading the words, with difficulty, from a blackboard.

"God made everything. He made our bodies and he planted our minds in them. He made the thunder roar and he bumped off old man Herménégilde. He made Sister Superior fart and he pulled one hair out of our heads every time we got a little older. One day I realized there's no more God up in Heaven than there's a snake with an electric bell in Québec. Heaven, the sky up there, is just a big empty box with a few shiny stones in it."

Ladouceur and Cassidy, cigars between their teeth, smiled. Phil filled his glass and pushed the bottle towards them.

He went on. "No more God, so I was all alone. When I was a kid they planted fears in me that grew as tall and thick as the corn in the garden. There was enough to feed on for the rest of my life. For eternity! Don't laugh, *baptême*! Without God I felt as if I'd been amputated, but I was a man, *hostie*! I could say, God doesn't exist but me, I exist. You haven't been born till you've said those words in the middle of the night, crossing Sainte-Catherine Street, weaving through the cars that whistle past your nose like scythes. Ah, for Christ's sake, listen to me . . . God doesn't exist, but me, I exist. I was breathing. It was *me* that was responsible for my own breathing."

He looked for his lighter, found it, looked for his cigars, chose one and surrounded himself with smoke.

"Sometimes an angel or one of the saints or even God himself used to come and nibble in the corner of my room like rats coming out of the sewer. Sometimes I could feel their little paws running across my chest in a panic when I couldn't get to sleep."

"You said there wasn't any God," the ironic Ted Ladouceur reminded him.

Phil laughed scornfully. He threw the bottle of Scotch at Cassidy who caught it and refilled the glasses.

Roch Carrier

"Trying to talk philosophy to you," said Phil, "is like trying to put lace underpants on a mare."

Cassidy and Ladouceur folded their stranglers' hands like perfect choir-boys. Heads bowed, in a monastic voice, they murmured, "Amen."

Reflect prejudices of most people in french Canada

* * *

The day had to come. Phil's fingers found no more money under the piles of folded clothing in his dresser drawers. He tossed the clothes on the bed, unfolded and shook them and emptied every drawer. Not a single dollar. He had exhausted his savings a long time ago and now he possessed absolutely nothing. His rings? He'd sell them.

The Craig Street Jew offered him a ridiculously low price, an insult. He was a thief. It would be better to be fleeced than go back to work. Ah! Why hadn't he followed Boris Rataploffsky in the rowboat into the water of the beautiful lake at Saint-Benoit-de-Beauce? Montreal was as dry as a stone.

While the old Jew had his nose in the cash-register Philibert picked up a pale blue plastic radio and stuck it in his jacket. He had his revenge.

If he could rob a Jew he wouldn't have to give up hope altogether. Perhaps he would even get rich.

Outside on the sidewalk he pressed the radio against him, being very careful not to look like a thief. The police protected the Jews because the Jews controlled the police and the governments and the businesses. Everybody knew that the Jews even controlled the *Anglais*. Ah, why wasn't he a Jew?

"It wouldn't be as hard as being a lousy stinking French Canadian. The Jews are rich and we haven't got gas ovens in Québec so they've got all the security they want. If we did have gas ovens they'd be the ones that sold them. Ah, those *maudits Juifs!*"

Farther long the street another old Jew in another shop agreed, after much bartering, to buy his radio for two dollars.

The time when life had been generous was closed behind him, like a big door that would never open again.

The Ninth Wonder of the World was dead. The dream was over.

If Phil went on like this he would have to sell his alligator shoes and his blue suit with the pink and green threads.

* * *

Bulldozers were snoring. Philibert didn't hear them any more than he heard the sound of his own breathing or the intermittent barking of the explosions that shook the bedrock.

Something wet hit him in the face: bird-shit? He looked up but he could see neither sky nor bird. Only the scaffolding criss-crossing over a steel frame. He wiped his face with the back of his hand. It was sticky with blood.

"*Tabernacle*!" yelled the man next to him. "It's skin off a man! "

"Yeah, because women are scarce *en hostie* around here!"

Other men working around them had been hit by bloody droplets too. Shovels were put down, hammers and picks fell to the ground. The workmen wiped their faces, looking around to find the source of the still-living bits of flesh that had spattered them.

The foreman burst out like another explosion.

"Bunch of goddamn lazy buggers, get back to work. You could at least earn enough to pay for the paper your cheques are printed on. I'll cut a quarter hour off your time, *bande de Christ*!"

Philibert bent down to pick up his shovel and held it up by the handle.

"You're a bigger pig than an *hostie* of a pig!"

"I do my job," said the foreman. "When I had to dig, I dug, no crybaby stuff. Now my job is giving you guys shit. I give you shit and you're going to do your work, *bande de Christ*! The Dominion Company isn't going to go broke here because of a *baptême* of a lazy bum like you!"

"Boss! Hey boss," shouted the man from the Beauce, sliding down the ladder. "It's the Portuguese guy. He blew up!"

"I'm telling you cows, *bande de Christ,* if you weren't so lazy maybe you'd be a little more careful and there wouldn't be all these accidents. What's Dominion going to say now?"

When the foreman was nervous he kept taking his cap off and putting it back on his head.

"Boss! Hey boss!" the *Beauceron* repeated. "It is not an accident, he put a stick of dynamite between his teeth and another one between his legs. We were laughing, thought it was a big joke, then he pressed the detonator and we kept on laughing because we thought, it won't go off, but it went off. We didn't see it, it happened too fast, but we didn't laugh any more. There isn't enough of him left to bury now."

"Why did that *Christ* of a DP have to go and do a thing like that? Canada gets too many of these starving Europeans. They come over here and take our jobs and as soon as they've got a full belly they blow themselves up."

"Then we get their crap in our faces," said a welder who was still cleaning himself off.

The foreman took off his cap and put it back on his head. "Why did he do it?"

"Crazy," suggested another welder.

"Crazy," repeated the foreman. "That's the only thing that could account for it."

Philibert threw down his shovel. "Crazy! Boss, we're the crazy ones. We're crazier than the goddamn crazies. If we weren't crazy we'd do like the Portuguese guy and this *baptême* of a pile of scrap iron we're sewing up for the rich guys would be fertilized by a flood of human meat chopped up by dynamite. But we're crazy, by Christ. If the rich guys want a castle, we build them one. That Portuguese guy wasn't crazy. He said, take your castle and shove it up your perfumed ass. Expensive perfume too. I couldn't even afford to put it on my face."

The foreman's hat danced off his head and back but he said nothing. Philibert didn't add a word. He went over to the beam where he had hung his jacket. He didn't pick it up. It was spotted with blood. The police on Sainte-Catherine Street would think he was a murderer.

"You, some day your craziness is going to catch up with you," said the foreman. "One of these days we're going to find *you* with dynamite in your mouth."

"Don't worry, boss. My craziness is taking this bitch of a life with a smile and then saying thank-you for it."

He wandered the streets aimlessly.

He walked.

Night fell.

Alone in his bed, despite his closed eyes and the heavy curtain at the window, Philibert could not erase the image of a chopped-up face, bleeding, whose laugh was a wound. The face was so disfigured he could not be certain that it was his own.

* * *

How many days had it been since Philibert had seen the springtime sky from the bottom of his grease-pit? He often dreamed of trips he had taken on beautiful sunny days, on highways that took him from the

Laurentians to the Appalachians, from the salty Gaspé air to the dry forests of Val d'Or. Now his horizon was restricted by the sticky walls of his grease-pit. Above him there was a sky of muddy tin and rusty pipes that spat out noxious clouds. Philibert coughed and spat. Grey water, grease and oil rained down on him. His coverall and shirt were soaked. No matter how vigorously he scrubbed himself his body left an oily outline on the sheets. The smell of gas and oil followed him; he could smell it everywhere like a stinking cloud from which he could not separate himself.

It was night when he finished work, and the night was invaded by automobiles that slithered along the streets like disgusting illuminated snakes.

One day a letter, stained by greasy hands, fell into Philibert's pit. It had been a long time since he had received a letter. Who could be thinking of him? It came from Morin, Morin, Morin and Morin, barristers and notaries.

"*Baptême*! Now the law's after me. I didn't do anything wrong."

He read it with feverish excitement.

Dear Sir:
  Will you kindly come to our offices in connection with the death of our client M. Donato Ambrosio, alias Louis Durand, alias Agadad Aglagayan, alias Jean-Baptiste Turcotte, alias Boris Rataploffsky *et alii* whom it appears that you knew by one of these names or another.
Yours very truly,

The signature was illegible.

"*Baptême*! They're going to make me pay for the coffin for the Ninth Wonder of the World. He didn't need a coffin, he needed a steamboat. They'll ruin me, but I don't care, I'll borrow the money. I'll buy flowers too."

* * *

Philibert had never seen so many books. The house seemed to be built not of bricks or stone but of books.

"Have you read that, *Monsieur le Notaire*?"

The man of law was so clean. No speck of dust, no vulgar word had come near him since his birth.

"No, alas, I have not read everything. One reads, one reads, then one realizes that one learns nothing more. One stops reading. But one continues to haunt the book-shops."

"Jesus, *Monsieur le Notaire,* you wouldn't talk like that if you'd gone to the kick-in-the-pants university."

"One must be determined, young man, and patient, patient. And one must have good will, know when to be quiet. A little luck helps too, of course. But that is something that *you* don't lack for."

"*Baptême, Monsieur le Docteur,* you don't know me very well."

The short bald man smiled—weakly, so as not to disturb the hairs of his moustache.

"Listen."

In a voice accustomed to appearing indifferent to good news and bad, the voice of an obsequious dead man careful not to awaken his neighbours, he began to read, pronouncing words and words and more words. Philibert did not understand a thing, only words piled on words. Suddenly, in the flow of dull verbiage, Philibert made out, "Consequently, Monsieur Phil, my manager, will inherit . . . ."

"Not so fast, *Monsieur le Curé!*"

The notary looked up from his papers without raising his head. "Monsieur, I lack sufficient holiness to be a *Curé* despite my honesty on which you can most assuredly depend."

"What am I inheriting, *Monsieur le Notaire*? Debts from the Ninth Wonder of the World?"

"Boris Rataploffsky, since that is the name by which you knew him, did not leave you a fortune . . . ."

"*Baptême!*" Philibert interrupted. "What *did* he give me?"

"He has left you an interesting sum, a very interesting sum I might say, one that you might profitably invest, following the expert advice of our brokerage office."

Philibert did not understand.

"Only if you wish to do so, of course," the notary specified.

Philibert ran to the door. He couldn't listen to another word.

"I'll be back, doctor. But before I come back I've got to go and get drunk. On credit, but I got to do it.

One last time. When you're rich you get drunk on champagne, but me, I like beer."

* * *

"I'm an heir!"

Philibert's old '37 Chevrolet was quivering like a child with a new toy. His foot trembled on the accelerator. His hands on the steering-wheel were trembling too, as though he were frightened.

"I'm an heir! An heir!"

He thought he was thinking of a hundred things, but these were the only words that came to his lips.

On the back seat of his car — was that why he was trembling? — he felt the breathing of something enormous, the breath of the Ninth Wonder of the World.

"You're my truly son. You're my boy. Don't forget," the gruff voice murmured very tenderly.

Philibert stopped the Chevrolet. He could not see anything. There were too many tears in his eyes.

"No, *Monsieur le géant*, I won't get drunk after all."

"You are good son," said the voice in the shadow of the Chevrolet.

He was no longer able to drive.

He crossed his arms on the steering-wheel and buried his head there, as though it were a pillow on which he could abandon himself to his sorrow.

Why had the Ninth Wonder of the World left him this inheritance? Was the giant all alone in the world? As alone as Philibert? Why had he ended his life in that ridiculous little rowboat? Why had he gone without a word of explanation to anyone, not even his manager?

"Deep down, you are good boy," said the voice in the back. Although the voice resembled that of the Ninth Wonder of the World, Philibert recognized his father's voice too.

"Father! I'm going to go and see you in the village and you're going to be proud of me. You won't want to boot my ass any more. When you see me you're going to take me in your arms."

He stepped firmly on the starter and drove his beat-up old car in the direction of the notary's office. The car responded like a stubborn mule. He pushed the accelerator to the floor, thinking crazily that he'd like to have a whip to make his car, his old old car, hurry up.

* * *

Philibert would be a grocer. A little grocery-store as clean as a house, with jars of jam arranged in multi-coloured pyramids and dusted every day. A grocery store that smelled good, big with a big front window.

His hands would be clean. He would use a white towel frequently to wipe them on. He would wear a white shirt and a blue or red bow-tie. The walls would be white too. The ceiling might be a bright pink colour. He would swallow his bad language in front of his

91

customers because he would be a respectable grocer. He would be polite. After they had done their shopping he would escort the customers to the door and he would be careful not to pinch their bums. The store would be called "Boris and Philibert." No. "Boris and Son"? No. "Rataploffsky and Associate"? No, that sounded too Jewish. Anyway, the name painted on the front of the store wasn't very important, the basic truth was written in his soul: he owed his life to the Ninth Wonder of the World. He would enroll in a night course to learn English, because English was the language of business, big business and monkey business. If you can't speak English you can't even take a leak when you want to. He would subscribe to English magazines like the office workers he'd seen on the bus. Those magazines told you things. *Baptême!* They had great pictures of naked women to give you some energy too. Then he would take a course in accounting because when he went to school they had taught him how to go to Heaven but not how to go to the bank. Before he became the manager of the Ninth Wonder of the World he couldn't even tell a profit from a loss. If he ran the grocery store well it would grow and prosper. Then later, perhaps he would . . . He didn't even dare think about it. Go into politics . . . He mustn't think about it. Politics . . . It was forbidden to think about it: he might as well dream of having a prick as big as a locomotive. *Baptême!* He might as well dream of having the wings of an angel. But if he became a big grocer, well, he'd be just as good as a lawyer, and maybe he could be an MLA . . .

"You, you've got the makings of a Prime Minister," an old man in a factory had once told him.

He would be a grocer. A nice little grocery store, all clean and neat and smelling good.

Before he bought his grocery store Philibert would go to the bank to deposit his inheritance. It was a long time since he had gone to the Savings Bank. Not since his unsuccessful rendezvous with the pretty little cashier.

If she was still behind her wicket he would hold out his cheque quite indifferently. She would be uncomfortable because she would remember turning up her nose at Philibert. She would look like a cat that has made a mess on the rug. She wouldn't dare look him in the eye. She would hide her eyes in her statements. She would pretend to have forgotten. Unhappy, she would be even prettier, with a beauty that would make a man happy to be a man and make him want to be good and strong, in love with life. Phil would not be ashamed to look her in the eye. He had nothing to blame himself for. His only fault was having been poor. He would ask her out. She would accept. Her woman's heart would know that Phil was capable of love. She would get into his old Chevrolet as though it were the carriage of a king. Say what you like, what a woman wants most from a man is love. To love . . .

"Ah! To love . . . to love . . . to love . . ."

* * *

The night was ripped open.

The burning of a whip in the flesh of his back.

A phosphorescent tree sprang into the windshield.

The dark wave of night fell again and the clamour of Montreal, near as it was, did not disturb the silence.

In the depth of the night the '37 Chevrolet had turned over. The wheels were spinning furiously.

* * *

The phosphorescent Cross of Christ rose up before Philibert like a tree on the road in front of his car. The outstretched arms sparkled like glowing coals and the gaping wound in the side of Christ was as broad as a neon city. He slammed on the brake but the wheels didn't bite the road and the car didn't cling to the pavement. It sank like a sword into the side of Christ and a tide of blood poured down on the windshield. The wipers managed to clear a semi-circle, but it was no use; their mechanism had broken down. Blood soaked the upholstery, flowed onto the seats, stained Phil's suit and trickled into his hair and onto his face. The warm blood ran onto his eyelids and his eyes, and the car was filled with the blood of Christ.

He pushed at the door with his shoulder, trying to get out, but the blood was running like a river and the roof of the car was shining above the red tide. Phil swam towards a shore that must exist somewhere. He had not been swimming since the muddy water of the little Famine River.

At the end of his strength, and heavier than a rock, he got back into the car which was breathed in, swallowed up, by a whirlpool.

His shouts were useless. The night was deserted and the distant windows on the other shore of night were deaf. A strong gust dragged him under the surface of the wave. Phil struggled, waving his arms and legs, and he managed to come up to the red surface. In the sky, stretching as far as he could see, was the gash in the side of Christ. Blood gushed in a torrent that was more tumultuous than Niagara. Blood poured over the mountains, tore up villages, inundated the city. The sea opened great blood-shot eyes.

The blood burned the harvests, carried off trees and rocks, uprooted skyscrapers. Phil could no longer struggle. His efforts had exhausted him. A man alone can do nothing. He closed his eyes, pressed his lips together, stretched his arms out along his body and accepted his own drowning with no anger or regret. He no longer had the strength to refuse.

While he was stretched out there across the blood that had become as diaphanous as fresh water, he noticed, up high, a man. It was a tight-rope walker, advancing cautiously along a wire stretched out in the sky, above the abyss of the night. The man slid his foot along the wire without lifting it. His arms were out-stretched, his body very stiff. The man was staring at a distant point in the night.

"Help!" Philibert called.

At the cry the tight-rope walker turned his head. The wire was shaken, the man tossed over. He lost his footing and fell, a wingless bird.

Phil's head was split open by the impact.

* * *

Phil opened his lips and a trickle of blood poured down onto his chin. He thought he had uttered the word "LIVE." The night trembled like a contented animal. It was a beautiful word, beautiful like a horse galloping across a field. The walls of night spoke with Phil's voice, repeating the word "LIVE."

His lips were open. Now no sound burst from his mouth. His throat was closed as though a hand were around his neck, strangling him.

* * *

Through the shattered windshield of his car Phil could see his limbs spread out in the night. A torn-off arm was a red flower. A leg looked like a broken branch and his head was surrounded by the water of a pool.

His body was scattered in the abyss of a dead memory.

* * *

Steel teeth, wide as doors, forever closed.
The jaws of hell.

When he was a child Philibert used to open the book at the page where they talked about hell and spend hours looking at the drawings of the open-mouthed dragon whose stomach led to Hell.

The jaws of hell.

Philibert used to spend a lot of time looking at the picture, frightening himself. He wanted his soul to be marked by fear, to be deeply scarred by it. The more scared he was the less he would feel like sinning.

The jaws of Hell.

Sometimes Philibert fell asleep on his open book and gently, lovingly, the dragon in the drawing would begin to lick his face.

Here are the jaws of Hell. At the edges of the lips, like spaghetti, but sickeningly slimy, serpents were swimming. The mere sight of them would drive a person mad, but in Hell one does not go mad and one cannot die of fear. Phil gave in to the giant worm's slimy caress as it twined itself around him. The burning of the fire was gentle compared to the serpent's caress. The filthy wetness of its sticky flesh pressed against him and its cold body smelled like vomit. The serpent wound around his ankles, tied itself there, gripped his legs and attacked them, encircled his thighs, his hips, pressed against his abdomen. Phil was no longer able to breathe. The serpent compressed his chest, preventing his lungs from expanding. Phil saw the serpent's face come closer, as though to tear out his eyes. But it rested against his cheek, pressing its cheek against Phil's, drooling. Revoltingly affectionate, the lips with their smell of rotten meat clung to Phil's lips like a bloodsucker. The serpent's tongue uncurled in his mouth and moved there like another serpent, like a maddened viper, sounding the depth of his throat.

Phil choked. The serpent's tongue slid into his throat. He must swallow the horrible living spit. The serpent's snout was now forcing open the ring of his mouth. Little by little the head moved into his mouth and insinuated itself into his throat. The head sank into Phil's chest like a stake, digging its way through the lungs. It dug through the liver, pierced the stomach, rippled through the intestines. Then it hesitated, rested a bit, hiccuped. Its belly growled and Phil thought it was his own. The serpent moved into his rectum. It wriggled through Phil's body as it had in its natal mud. Phil's stomach rotted until it looked like the belly of a dead cow in the wheatfield. The serpent stretched his anus, its head came out and Phil could feel the bumps on its skull, feel the head dangling between his legs like a miscarried foetus. The neck stretched, the head rose and the mouth took hold of Phil's penis. The jaws closed around it. Under his feet and along his thighs the agony of the flames was sweet. He did not feel the pebbles of fire.

All that remained of him was an enormous suffering, a pain that would last through eternity, a pain that would suffer pain, that would prolong its torments longer than it would take the wings of a bird to wear out all the rocks in the world.

"Suffer. Suffer to suffer. Suffer to suffer. Suffer to suffer. Suffer. Suffer."

Phil managed to see through the half-light where the grating voice originated. The shadow did not completely veil a hare-lipped face. The sad features seemed on the verge of tears.

A little snake slid out of the deep-set eye like a tear.

"To be alive is a curse."

The words awakened a snake in its nest. It came out the other socket.

"I never asked to live," said Phil.

A thin pig's head moved on a skeleton whose bones looked like a calcified shrub. The monster threw itself among the burning coals on all four feet, barked, and jostled the serpent like a boisterous pup.

"You are suffering," he said mockingly. "You have always wanted to suffer."

The flames were stirred by the movements of the maddened creatures and the earth decomposed in jagged sparks, but the fire darkened, the flames turning grey. The light was dusty and no longer held back the night, which became entirely black again. The untouchable black vault of the sky hurtled down on Phil, and the weight of that cartload of bricks overturned on him.

*   *   *

The night felt warm to him, like a mother. He was alone, but where? In his childhood bed, perhaps; his heart stopped because there was a hand on his chest. His heart was a little berry between big iron fingers.

On the overturned car a wheel that was still alive lost momentum as the blood flowed out. It weighed against the axle, slowed down, hesitated, turned again, barely turned, weakened, moved sluggishly, stopped.

Philibert thought he said, "Is that the sun?"

House of Anansi Fiction (in print)